The wraith-woman reached out for Tess Goodraven, who stood before her, straining to see. Tess stumbled back. In the stabbing rain and blinding flashes of lightning, she could not be sure she had actually seen the wraith approaching amid the gravestones.

Tess twisted her body, her boots firmly set in the mud. In the thunderstorm's white pulses, she could see the whole Salem graveyard lit up, and there behind her, the comforting figure of Tobias.

He stood staring ahead like a man mesmerized by a magician. Had he seen it? She had no time to speak before she felt the unmistakable touch of a spirit. Tiny pinpricks of ice fell upon her neck, and her heart seemed to stop for an instant. Mist gathered sleepily around her, swirling in the gusts of wind.

Around the muddy hem of her dress, the mist slowly spun, low and thick, with Tess in the center of its motion. The fog had a quality, an indefinable life within it, an *intention*.

The mist, the spirit-creature, closed in around her, and suddenly Tess perceived the wraith's urgency. It was not just anger she was giving off. It was need.

Spirit

J. P. HIGHTMAN

HARPER TEEN
An Imprint of HarperCollinsPublishers

HarperTeen is an imprint of HarperCollins Publishers.

Spirit
Copyright © 2008 by J. P. Hightman

10 East 53rd Street,
New York, NY 10022.
www.harperteen.com
Library of Congress Cataloging-in-Publication Data
Hightman, Jason.
    Spirit / by J. P. Hightman. — 1st ed.
        p.   cm.
    Summary: In 1892, a wealthy, seventeen-year-old, married couple, Tess and Tobias
Goodraven, lay ghosts to rest for the thrill of it but, separated by the terrible witch who was
responsible for the Salem witchcraft horrors, they may not have strength to survive, much less
help the dead.
    ISBN 978-0-06-085065-4
    [1. Witchcraft—Fiction.   2. Ghosts—Fiction.   3. Love—Fiction.   4. Supernatural—
Fiction.   5. Massachusetts—History—19th century—Fiction.   6. Salem (Mass.)—History—
Colonial period, ca. 1600–1775.]   I. Title.
PZ7.H543995Spi   2008   2007041934
[Fic]—dc22   CIP
                                                                                    AC

Typography by Hilary Zarycky
    09   10   11   12   13   LP/RRDH   10 9 8 7 6 5 4 3 2 1
❖
First paperback edition

As always, to Kim and to my family.

With deep thanks to my talented,
skillful, patient editor,
Ruth Katcher

PREFACE

These are not the Salem witches you know.

The objects under consideration in these pages are not the innocent men and women caught up in the Salem trials—born of hysteria and hate—but rather, the real and true thing.

Much has been written of the witch trials. But there were other trials, later and less famous, in the Massachusetts township. It was left to secret judges and tribunals to deal with the real forces of darkness in that terrible age.

This story reaches back many centuries, and no doubt will reach forward many more, but the first serious investigation into the true Salem magicians began in the Victorian period.

PROLOGUE

The Salem Woods

1892

❧❧

Winter breathed upon her.

The morning was cold, as it had been yesterday, and the day before that. The girl's coat was not thick enough, but she said nothing to her father. His job was to inspect the rails before the train from Salem to Blackthorne went through for the first time in ages. He had taken her along, because his wife had passed on, and there was no one to watch over the honor of a fifteen-year-old girl, and he disliked the rough young men eyeing her at the bakery, where she'd bought a meager breakfast.

She was unhappy, but did not complain. She could ensure he finished the task, for he was known to be lax, a wanderer, fond of whiskey, who could not hold employment. They were lucky to have any money in their pockets. Eighteen ninety-two had been a hard year, with little to look forward to. Truth be told, the two of them could wander off into the landscape and never return, and no one would be surprised.

They were completely alone on the railbed that ran along the snowy forest, joined only by the sound of his long metal cane tapping at the tracks.

She wandered a few feet into the woods after an animal,

perhaps a deer, though it seemed larger, some dark thing moving among the snowdrifts in this bitter patch of wilderness not far from Blackthorne. It was low to the ground, like a shadow, and slipped with terrible, silent grace beyond view, the feathery snow and the trees conspiring to create a veil.

It was then she noticed the tapping had ceased.

When she turned, she saw her father had stopped. His gaze seemed to fix upon her, and even at this distance she could see his face carried no expression whatsoever. For a very long moment, unsure of his meaning, she simply returned his look, drawn mysteriously into a sense of growing fear. She glanced behind her and saw no threat that could have taken his attention. He had about him a completely alien intensity, a predatorial aspect, as when a dog stiffens before moving into attack. He carried the metal cane in one hand and he remained motionless, even his eyes, still, unblinking.

What have I done, she thought desperately. But she could think of nothing. She called to him, but he gave no reaction at all.

He stayed unmoving for so long that finally she began plodding toward him, her feet stinging with the cold in worn-down boots. Stopping not a foot in front of him, she saw a foreign presence in his eyes. A blue smoke drifted across his pupils as if he were somehow burning within.

Then something changed in the air. His head turned to the forest, as if recognizing some new arrival she could not see in the snow flurries. A crackling sound cut across the woods, and for just an instant her father was overcome with white vines of electricity, as if he were covered by a luminous ivy that had grown up from the ground, but was gone again in a blink, leaving only a charred smell.

His hand slowly came forward and took hers into an iron grip. She was suddenly aware of a thick azure mist rising from the snow around the tracks. Again she spoke urgently to her father, and again he said nothing.

The mist dissipated around him. She wanted to scream, but could not. And then, still saying nothing, he walked her calmly but firmly onto a great sheet of ice, a frozen lake that lay beside the tracks.

They stood on the frozen waters together, and she asked him what was wrong, begging for an answer. He did not reply, but instead raised his metal cane above his head with a heavy grunt, and then brutally brought it down onto the ice. She tried to run, but he held her to the spot.

He cracked open the frozen lake and pulled her down with him into the black water.

The Home of the Ghosthunters,
A Drawing Room, New York City, 1892

CHAPTER ONE
⚜

H*ere we are again,* Tess was thinking.

Tess and Tobias Goodraven, in their mahogany chairs, facing each other near the bay windows, cellos at the ready, and now beginning to play. The petite young lady, dressed in white, dark hair in a perfect coil behind her head, and the light-haired young man, dashing but unkempt, were again building a musical wall between themselves and the world.

The room was large and its two occupants might have looked fragile beneath the high ceiling, but to Tess this was the safest and friendliest of places, even in the midst of an argument.

Neither spoke. They let their cellos do the talking. The low throbbing of the strings, like a prisoner humming a dirge, reverberated off the portraits, the antiquities, the dark emerald wallpaper and the black wood of the floor, and wrapped the couple in a cocoon of their own making.

Such gloomy noises fit perfectly in the Goodraven mansion.

The room was lined with dusty books, overflowing from the library, volumes filled with the sinister ramblings of forgotten men, accounts of travels made in the worst of times to places never meant to be visited—all stories Tobias had paged through, but never finished, each time driven to a new one, or to his maps, or into his own investigations.

His restlessness was exciting to Tess, and wearying, and often she couldn't decide which she felt more.

The music moved through her entire body as she held the cello between her knees, the instrument's long swanlike neck rising beside her head, its strings digging pleasantly into her fingers.

She was never going to admit she'd been wrong.

To look at her, you would never have known she had such a rebellious spirit. She seemed much the same as any pretty, upper-class woman in the city, but spend two minutes in conversation with her, and her devilish playfulness and desire to shock the prim sensibilities around her would be obvious.

She was more than matched in this by Tobias, who forever relished in playing the scoundrel.

They had been married less than a year.

This was their first real disagreement, though his silence was not unusual; he seemed to crave it at times. But the music often healed him, brought him back to her.

Her playing had become a mere scraping of the strings. She regained her concentration, but too late. Tobias furrowed his brow, noting her distraction, answering her trills with his own. He was a tall, slim gentleman, Tobias was, with a handsome, rounded face that softened the impression made by his shockingly white hair. Those snowy, fine angelic strands often fell forward over bored, faded green eyes that lit up whenever something morbid or novel presented itself.

Because as a rule he was so humorous, Tess half expected him to smile at any moment, but he was altogether different when he was immersed in playing. He'd make no exception today.

It was a quiet, ancient piece, moody in the extreme, the kind Tobias usually favored, full of contemplation, never quite giving in to the melody. The music conjured up images of reverberant chambers in a decaying castle, in a time of plagues and sorrows, with the dead piling up in the streets, while behind the high gates of a fortress, the approval of a lovelorn nobleman was all that concerned the court musicians. (At least, this is what floated into Tess's mind.)

Tobias played the more difficult, lower bass line, investigating a rich darkness Tess would never dare to reach, exploring a cold emptiness she would fear. His eyes fell closed.

Now the couple departed from the written notes, and instead joined each other in finding new ground. Tobias had a genius for this. His improvisations perfectly matched her higher wanderings, the two streaming lines of music separating and harmonizing. Though Tess was not always certain of *his* next moves, he knew exactly where she was going, and met her there with a chivalrous echo, playfully teasing out her adventurousness, drawing from her new pleadings. He continually surprised her, and pleasantly so.

He dominated her now, taking over the slight melody and moving the music into a territory more bleak than any Gothic landscape, and she accompanied him with a plain bowing.

She had a tendency to follow him wherever he went, in music, as in life.

The Goodravens were unique, and they knew it, and they enjoyed it. Not many seventeen-year-olds were so rich, or lived on their own in a mansion, with a butler and house staff to do whatever they wanted; not many people their age were married; and very few hunted ghosts just for the thrill of it. Their lives were magical. And dangerous beyond measure.

Tess had a small but growing awareness of this danger.

She had begun to worry about where this witches' trail was going to take them.

"Are you ready to talk about it yet?" she inquired, somewhat playful. Lately their music had often preceded deep and wide-ranging discussions.

But he didn't look up. He made his bow strikes a bit angrier, slicing out a quicker tempo. No, he was not ready to talk.

The "incident" in the Salem graveyard several nights ago had been something more than the quiet séances they'd joined in New England, more than the gentle sensing of spirits they'd observed in their journeys in Europe, or even in distant India, where they had witnessed the moving of furniture all on its own in a British ambassador's residence.

This Salem business was considerably more aggressive.

Tess moved her eyes past Tobias to the bay windows and a solemn brownstone building adorned with grim, overfed gargoyles. She could dimly hear the ragged clatter of hooves, and coachmen sniping at each other and their horses, trying to steer a clear path. The second-floor parlor did not allow a view of the Manhattan street below, but Tess had imprinted the avenue in her mind's eye: darkly dressed men, in top hats and bowlers, high collars smudged with ink by the end of the day, and the light, at the dinner hour, drifting lazily down through billows of smoke. The windows were thick, but she was faintly aware of them, could *feel* their bitter mélange of tired-out resentment.

The muffled sensation, a low-burning plaintive anger, of men wanting something better, drifted upward, pressing on Tess, as if a weight had been laid upon her back. She'd have blocked it out if it were possible. But the feelings of others radiated, floated, and permeated the air immediately around them inescapably. Tobias shared her odd ability to pick up on these stirrings, but the effects seemed to toughen him, causing him to view them as entertainments, while she tended to take on ever more sympathy, more pain, more worry, for others, for the unfortunates of the world.

Now his long, agile fingers bent the strings to a demanding rise in melody, as her hand fell, finishing with a descending elegance.

His voice intruded on the silence.

"So what exactly is it you want to talk about, Tess? Is there something I need to set right?" he asked, lightening his brooding expression, as if ready to grin.

She paused. Keeping a straight face, knowing he could read her every emotion, she said, "Tobias, I'm not asking for an apology for your sharp remarks, which I am overlooking with characteristic grace and a heroic lack of self-pity. But I'd like you to admit the situation in the Salem graveyard was more frightening than you had expected."

"Of course it was. And it was fantastic."

Tess refused to smile. "Something awful could have happened to us."

"That's the general idea of adventuring, my dear."

"That thing was monstrous."

He made himself look appalled. "Dearest Tess, are you and I remembering the same night?"

CHAPTER TWO

T hey had come on a mission to aid the dead, but the Goodravens instead discovered an angry, disoriented phantom. Her ghostly form, bones visible under skin, glided through the rainstorm, mist upon mist, whispers within whispers. She—it—emerged from the blackness, and then lost all shape and definition, dissipating into nothingness.

The wraith-woman reached out for Tess Goodraven, who stood before her, straining to see the vanishing likeness. Tess stumbled back. In the stabbing rain and blinding flashes of lightning, she could not be sure she had actually seen the wraith approaching amid the gravestones.

Tess twisted her body, her boots firmly set in the mud. In the thunderstorm's white pulses, she could see the whole Salem graveyard lit up, and there behind her, the comforting figure of Tobias.

He stood staring ahead like a man mesmerized by a magician. Had he seen it? She had no time to speak before she felt the unmistakable touch of a spirit. Tiny pinpricks of ice fell upon her neck, and her heart seemed to stop for an instant. Mist gathered sleepily around her, swirling in the gusts of wind.

Around the muddy hem of her dress, the mist slowly spun, low and thick, with Tess in the center of its motion.

She stared at Tobias, who watched with blank fascination, perhaps even jealousy. The fog had a quality, an indefinable life within it, an *intention*.

The mist, the spirit-creature, closed in around her, and suddenly Tess perceived the wraith's urgency. It was not just anger she was giving off. It was need.

Tobias's hand thrust into the mist, and he pulled Tess out of the rising column before the wraith's aim could be fully known.

"Step clear of the grave," he said. Tess fell back behind Tobias, and watched in the scatterlight as he confronted the empty fog: "Mary, stop—we've not come to disturb you. I've brought back what was stolen. . . ."

Perhaps at the sound of its name, the Wraith halted, the mist seemingly frozen in the air.

Tobias reached back, pulling from the darkness a small cedar box. He slid it open, revealing a collection of skeletal fragments.

"They're your bones, Mary. *Your* bones. I've found them," Tobias called.

For just an instant, the thing near the open grave became mortally realized and took on a female appearance, almost an innocence: a Puritan lady in tattered clothes. But at that instant Tobias slipped on the dirt mound where he stood, and suddenly the box slid loose from his fingers, the skeleton pieces tumbling *into the grave,* falling past the Wraith-woman, who seemed to feel the passage of her very bones through her. And then she was gone, as if obliterated by the shock of it.

Tobias recovered, perched on the edge of the gravesite, and turned to see that Tess was safe. She looked down, wide-eyed, into the darkness of the pit below.

"Bury it," Tess uttered against the rain.

Within moments, the grave was covered in earth. Finished with the work, Tobias slammed a thin weathered headstone back into place that read:

MARY SUTTON

VICTIM OF THE SALEM WITCH TRIALS

DIED YOUNG 1692

And Tess exhaled with relief.

The bones, stolen ages ago by souvenir hunters, and tracked down with great difficulty by Tess and Tobias, had at last returned to their final resting place, precisely two centuries since the woman's death.

Exhausted, Tobias rose to stand by Tess, amid the rain-ravaged, broken gravestones. For a moment the storm calmed, and Tess heard water pattering off the ivy hanging on the forlorn statues of the marble angels. And then the calm was shattered as the headstone before them squealed and cracked, and gave out something like a breath.

A bluish mist emerged from the grave and instantly gathered body and fullness, the Puritan girl's spirit soaring free. It was the soul of Mary Sutton, reaching for the heavens, and as the phantom crossed through her, Tess again felt a deep chill, as if a frost had settled in her veins.

For an instant, their minds were one, Tess and the Puritan girl, and then the spirit moved on, passed into Tobias, and then lifted itself, or was lifted, upward, higher, faster, departing the living world.

Tess felt warmth return to her blood. The couple looked at each other, sharing the terrible awe and fear of the moment. Exhilarated. Stunned.

Tobias reached for Tess's hand.

"She is quieted," he said.

A few minutes later, huddled under an umbrella, Tess and Tobias stood near the cemetery's entrance and signaled their horse-drawn coach. Tess stared off into the distance. "She spoke to me. As she passed."

Tobias nodded, mulling it over. "She said there were others, others who weren't innocent. Fascinating, really. She had a stench to her, though, didn't she?"

Tess shut her eyes at the memory. "Decidedly."

"You there!" yelled a voice. A bearded, barrel-chested man carrying a lantern was rushing over the muddy field behind them. "What were you doing here? It's past midnight!"

Tobias calmly took a sociable tone. "That it is. And cold, too, in the rain. Offer us some warm spirits?"

Tobias had a way of getting what he wanted without being particularly charming. People simply yielded to him, Tess thought. He had shown her these past few years that often you get what you desire in life by bluntly telling people what you need and not asking at all.

But she was thankful for his forwardness as she sat in the

gravetender's warm cottage. Hard to call anything so small a house, but cozy it was, despite the presence of the dead who surrounded it.

The gravetender sat with Tobias and Tess at the table and the man's loneliness nearly drowned them, with much the same intensity as the downpour outside. His words spilled from a hoarse throat, seldom used.

"And you say you have a sickness?" he asked them now.

"I feel that's the brightest word for it," Tobias answered. "But we wouldn't want to burden you with the particulars of our unhappiness."

The man rubbed his beard with the tips of his dirty fingers, his eyes showing great concern. "Would it make me a braggart if I said I may be of help to you? Many's the time a visitor brought low by the facts of death has found comfort here."

To Tess's surprise, Tobias began to relate to the gravetender the circumstances of their life and history, lifting the curtain on their entire past. Both orphaned at thirteen by a terrible theater fire in Manhattan, the two had met in a church. For over a week they ate charity food, and slept in donated beds, among a dozen other unlucky orphans, overseen by dour nuns and clergymen while their families were notified. Tess had clung to Tobias, as there was a priest with a most disagreeable manner who seemed unduly interested in her whenever she found herself alone. And the other children seemed greatly disturbed, staring at her with a chilling dullness, hour after empty hour.

Tobias seemed the only one alive.

But they were destined to part. Eight days after the fiery

tragedy, an aging uncle from Maine came for Tobias, moving into the family home in New York. Tess was sent to live with her grandmother in Pennsylvania, watched by a governess in the echoing upper halls and lost rooms of the great house, where wallpaper dripped like the peeling skin of a corpse.

It was an unhappy time. Tobias was left alone for weeks on end, as his uncle spent every moment tending to business matters, while seemingly an eternity away, Tess's moody governess kept her from anyone who might bring her friendship or solace. Miss Lilly was an unmarried Southern woman who enjoyed the power of her position, and took up the management of Tess with fierce strictness. Perhaps due to this, Tess grew into a young lady of great composure—with a tendency to dislike restraint.

During that time, Tobias's letters kept her afloat, and her messages to him became warm conspiracies of escape.

Tobias narrated this story with great flair, the whole thing seeming as grim and dark as a dime novel. He couldn't help but embellish a few flavorful elements (the uncle keeping him in a tower next to a frothing idiotic cousin who smelled of urine was a complete invention on his part). But the tale came to a relatively happy ending: the uncle became senile and Tobias, with the help of a worried butler, had stuffed the old man away in a rural home under supervision. Tobias Goodraven thus became his own man, so to speak, at the age of sixteen.

Tess and Tobias had kept up their correspondence intensely for three years after the tragic fire in New York, until they met again at a séance. It was held in Manhattan at the request of a lawyer who'd lost his wife in the theater that night, and who felt the gathering would be more powerful if other survivors participated in trying to reach their lost loved ones. Few agreed, but Tess and Tobias—having experienced strange and growing sensitivities ever since the fire—were eager to see a true expert in the occult who might summon real results.

At the séance, their contact with the spirit realm was momentary but dramatic, a wave of invisible energy that fell upon them like unseen hands, followed by an intense heat. Faces appeared in the dim room. Then, astoundingly, the fire restarted itself right there in the psychic's chambers, sweeping up the curtains and nearly engulfing the medium as everyone fled the house. That touch with death had changed their lives almost as much as the theater fire itself, Tobias often said.

After this, Tobias enjoyed five long days of courtship with Tess, as she and her grandmother recovered from the séance. Miss Lilly had disagreed with the occult project from the start and remained at the hotel that night, but Grandmother had developed an interest in such things, missing Grandfather more and more over the years since his death.

It was at the end of that heady week, with her governess's willful disapproval, that Tess accepted Tobias's marriage proposal and began a new life in New York City. Certainly they were young, but such marriage was not unheard of, nor unlawful, nor unwise, if the match was a good one. Tess told herself that she and Tobias fit together, hand in glove; or cello by cello, for she took it as a great omen they both played the instrument. Everything had fallen into place, Tess thought now, as she sat in the graveyard house. She did miss Grandmother, so far away, but certainly not her retired governess; Tobias was all she needed. She could hardly believe it, but their anniversary would be in just weeks.

All of this Tobias told the gravetender, prattling on. Meanwhile, Tess was terribly aware of the rainwater in her stockings and boots, a dampness stubbornly unmoved by the gravetender's fire, and her impatience was growing. This mattered not a bit to Tobias, who seemed to have met his equal in late-night conversation. He was completely toying with the man, enjoying his reactions.

"The séance to find our parents was largely a success, and the ultimate result of this spirit visitation was," as Tobias put it, "a sickness that came to both of us. A shameful, unstoppable thirst for the *worst* that the world can offer."

The man at the table leaned back, a worrisome riddle in his eyes. "What is it that has a grip on you?"

"It's most unpleasant." Tobias sighed.

"I knew something was awry. There is a hollowness to your gaze. And the color of you both, like white ash."

Tobias nodded, looking regretful and wonderfully lost-lamby.

The man accepted his shame. "You poor wretches. There's no getting free of this sickness?"

"It is relentless. Our very blood begs us for satisfaction."

"And what is the name of your poison? Opium?"

"Worse than opium, sir."

"It has led us to this very place," interjected Tess.

"To a graveyard?"

Tobias leaned closer. "The digging up of graves is part and parcel of our sickness. We yearn for darkness. We . . . have a great love of phantoms, sir."

The man came in closer, as if his hearing had gone faulty. "What?"

Tobias answered him plainly. "We seek contact with the dead. We hunt lives lost."

"Your jesting is ill-mannered, sir."

"This is no joke, my good man. If you know of a way to be free of such wanting, I should be glad to hear your remedy."

The man still looked confused. "You came here to disturb ghosts?"

"And found one, I should say," replied Tess. "A ghost of Salem, and the old witch trials here."

Tobias leaped in, detailing his new interest in Salem after visiting the Boston Spiritualists Society. (Bostonians were always going on about the witch trials, and in gruesome detail.) "Our sort of crowd," said Tobias. "Corpse-lovers, every one of them."

"Do you realize the wrongness of meddling out here? I should call the police to snatch you up," said the gravetender distastefully. His words held a sadness, as if he wished to keep the couple from leaving, crazy or not. Tobias and Tess knew. They always had a strange, sharp awareness of the people around them. To say they were good judges of character would be an understatement. They had a *sense*.

"That dead woman had her bones stolen by some vile collector. We simply returned them. We did you a good turn," Tobias said, rising. "It's clear you have no sympathy for people in such circumstances as we find ourselves, so we will take our leave. I'm sorry we wasted our time. I thought you might have some wisdom to impart. Nonetheless, thank you for the . . . hospitality."

Tobias took Tess's arm and guided her to the door. For a minute it had seemed to her Tobias sincerely hoped the gravetender could help them in some way. But what wisdom could anyone have for such as they?

"Off with you, then," the gravetender grumbled. "You disturb the peace here. I've heard the spirits warn of terrible death for such as you. They whisper it, they howl it, these nights—'*Those who seek truth in the blood of Salem dead will find nothing but torment in their head. . . . From their loved ones, they shall be torn and severed, lost in hell, now and forever.*' Do you hear me?"

Tobias turned back to the man. "I'm shivering in my boots, sir. You have set us on the path to rightness with your words. Thank you, and good night."

Tobias helped Tess to get in the coach. "Quick-witted man," he said. "I can't speak for you, but I'm utterly terrified."

Tess took hold of the coach and climbed up wearily. The electric explosion of the spirit encounter had left her, and the ordinary world, with its ordinary feelings, had returned completely.

They'd had their adventure. Not just mist, but swirling mist; touching a spirit life of great power. Tired now, she hardly noticed the gravetender's ranting.

But the ghost's claim would stay in her mind for a long time after. *Not all of the accused were innocent.* Mary Sutton's spirit had wanted Tess to know this. Perhaps somehow she sensed Tess was special, unafraid of the darkness beyond the edge of life.

Of this darkness, Tess and Tobias Goodraven knew a great deal. They spent most of their time and fortune chasing nothing else but supernatural revelation. But this had been a special encounter, more real than ever before.

Tobias took her hand, almost apologetically. He was full of energy and would inevitably want to pursue the matter further. He would want to mount an investigation into the true Salem witches, and the shadows that grew in the heart of New England.

Five Days Later,
The Goodraven Mansion, New York, 1892

CHAPTER THREE
꠸

T hose who seek the truth in the blood of Salem dead will find
nothing but torment in their head. . . . Rather upsetting, Tess
thought now, unless the gravedigger had been making it all
up. She put it out of her mind.

Tess and Tobias remained in the parlor, facing each other, cellos
straight, bows fallen, discussing the danger they might confront if
they looked any further into the lives of the Salem witches. Despite
Tess's misgivings, she knew resistance would lead nowhere.

"The Unseen Ones . . . were not innocent, she said . . . ,"
mumbled Tobias, pondering the parting message of the graveyard
spirit. "How very, very interesting."

Chilled, and not just by the weakening fire, Tess half wished to
return to common, everyday interests—but nothing about her
life with Tobias was normal. Even the music they'd been playing
had been learned from an encounter with a ghost in Vienna.

She sighed. "Shall we speak of witches again, then?"

Visions of hellish engravings, page after page of tortured
witches, floated into her mind, illustrations from the books they
had been reading lately. "If you want to understand that cemetery
spirit, Tobias, we must retrace our path in history. Now, I don't

know about 'Unseen Ones' but witchcraft has always seemed an excuse for persecuting women . . . and pagans . . . and little more than that, as far as I'm concerned."

"Witchcraft," he repeated, turning the word in his head. "A way to power. Power to bewitch men."

"Power of flight."

"Broomsticks and black cats."

"Black candles and black magic."

Tobias's voice became distracted, lost in thought. "They said in Boston that the Salem witches could move things with just the exertion of the mind, project themselves to be in many places at once . . ."

"Nonsense. There were struggles in the church, mere infighting. Calling someone a witch was a perfect way to wrench the neck of an irritating rival. Where's the real mystery in it?" She remembered woodcut illustrations of women screaming in panic. Down through history, you could find eruptions in the boundless hatred of men toward women, or really, in the powerful toward the weak. She wished he didn't find the imagery so exciting.

"These young women of Salem were behaving as if possessed," Tobias argued.

"Well, witches made an easy scapegoat for any strange conduct—"

"Exactly. Which means there was strange conduct going on to begin with. *Something* caused their behavior, so what was it? Something was wrong with those girls."

"You're really not going to let us play today, are you?" Tess carefully set her cello against a bookcase.

"Go through the theories again. One at a time."

With a deep breath, Tess began. "One: The girls in Salem were hysterical, surrounded with crazed religious dogma, day in and out. Two: Perhaps they were faking possession by the devil. Once they started, they got more status and attention, and couldn't easily stop—"

"That spirit we saw in the graveyard did not seem hysterical. Or deceptive."

"But it passed through us quickly, and there were distractions. You can't discern facts from a ghost."

"In the accounts of the time, there was a slave woman who saw something."

"Please," said Tess. "That slave woman was trying to satisfy her master, saying what he wanted to hear. She was the only one not executed, because she cooperated . . . and because her owner would have lost his property—her. Who knows what she saw?"

"She spoke of seeing a devil in the woods."

"Insanity."

"But it's in the public record that she said it. Under oath. She spoke of the witches appearing and disappearing—"

"They were hallucinating, all of them there in Salem," she conjectured. "They were under the influence of a chemical that developed in the grain. Blood poisoning causes you to see things, you get crazed and feverish, you lapse into a coma—"

"Tess," he said doubtfully. "You mean to say the Salem witch trials were merely a case of bad food?"

"Well, don't you think it remarkable that wherever in history you find spooky, devilish tales and hysterical witch-hunting, you also seem to find this very problem with the grain?"

"Nobody else shares this view, among the experts," Tobias chided. "Is this all science has come up with?"

Science. Science was his new religion, as with everyone these days. Tess was at the end of her patience. "There are other, obvious possibilities, Tobias. Salem and all of New England had been through the Indian Wars. They'd seen bloodshed and scalping and terrible things, and these shocks and tragedies had wormed their way into their imaginations. They thought up witches to explain nightmarish visions that were really just violent memories."

"No," he said. "Something's missing."

"Turns out she was right," said a voice, and the couple turned to see their butler entering the room. Horrick was a portly man of fifty with reddish hair and beard, who looked rather like a worried orangutan.

"Who was right?" asked Tobias.

Horrick slammed down several books and old newspapers at a long table. "The spirit you met with at the graves. It spoke the truth. There *were* some who escaped the Salem witch trials. And I think I understand why your spirit called them 'the Unseen Ones.'"

CHAPTER FOUR

ore. How Tess and Tobias loved it.

Horrick knew they were captivated. "These escaped witches. When they left Salem, they went to a little town called Blackthorne."

Tess arched her back, trying to see what he'd brought, knowing she'd be the one who'd have to read through it in detail. "What have you got there?"

"Did your research for you, as usual," answered the butler. "These are old papers from the *Times* archive, original documents, letters, but this is the last of it."

Tobias stared. "The last of what, Horrick?"

"The last time I do this sort of thing." Horrick's voice descended, and he sent out a pervasive dread that Tess could pluck from the air. "It's bad for the soul, these things you have me look into—you and her gone off all the time, leaving me alone in this house, reading on all manner of horrifying calamities—"

Tobias was untroubled. "We count on you to dig this stuff up, Horrick. Double your salary."

"I can't do that, sir."

"Why not, Horrick?"

"I don't handle the money, the accountant does, excepting petty expenses."

"Then I'll have him deduct two dollars a week for your complaining all the time."

Tess looked at Tobias, bemused, and said, "Don't mind him, Horrick. If there's any good hauntings we haven't been to, he likes to be the one to find them."

"I always do find them," bragged Tobias. "He just fleshes out the details. In fact, Horrick, why exactly do we bother with you?"

Horrick sighed unhappily, familiar with the routine. "I'm not coming back, sir," the butler said solemnly. "If you go off looking for these spirits, I'll be done in this house. You engage in these hunts, and for no reason but for sport."

"All hunts are for sport, Horrick. Deduct two more dollars for your impertinence," ordered Tobias, and after Tess gave a disapproving look he said, "and add two dollars for your dramatic performance here."

"That still leaves me two dollars down, sir."

"And well it should." Tobias sighed. "What else did you find out?"

Horrick lifted a very old page among the stacks. "It's really quite an oddity," he said. "You see here some older papers on the Salem trials of 1692, journals and the like. Here the prosecutor listed the accused, but if you look . . ." He pointed to an ornamented space at the top of the page. "There was a first name. Behind all the others. A First Accused . . . who has been wiped out from history. Painted over. Unseen."

He then pulled over an old, tattered book. "It's not the only reference. Another journal states there were rituals observed around this person: terrible deaths, intestines ripped out of living bodies and come to life like snakes, strangling other men . . . fires that grew out of people's eyes . . . Quite shocking. She or he is listed only as Accused Number One. All this was recorded before the trials we know. . . . "

Tess withheld a shiver. "Caused by this unknown person?"

Horrick nodded. "The origin of all the hysteria. A First Witch."

Tobias tapped his bow on his chin. "We have no name?"

"No," said Tess, drawing closer. "Listen for a change."

"I'm an excellent listener," he said, distracted by the fluttering of a moth.

"Someday they're going to diagnose your condition. You can't pay attention for half a second," said Tess.

"Wish they'd diagnose my other condition," Tobias answered, snapping up the moth in his hand.

"And which sickness would that be? You've got thousands . . ."

"My sad and depressive states. Which you never help," said Tobias, pondering what to do with the insect.

Tess grinned at him. "You wouldn't survive a minute without me."

Tobias thought about it, and then nodded begrudgingly. "True. I suppose I wouldn't." Then he shut the moth in a book, smashing it and immediately wishing he hadn't. Tobias loved books. For living things, he had less concern.

Horrick, annoyed, began tapping the old court journal. "These records were doctored. Most likely by railroaders wanting to draw people back into town. . . . "

"The town of Blackthorne? The railroad has business that way?" Tobias asked.

"New business," answered Horrick, setting aside the ancient documents and pulling out a crisp newspaper. "This article clarifies a few things: Back in 1692 some of the accused in Salem ran away to Blackthorne and were killed there. Since then, the town has gone through every variety of misfortune. The place died out several times, in fact. In the early 1700s a plague drove everyone away; bad water was blamed. Then about twenty years ago they laid tracks there, but some kind of accident scared the investors off. But now there's interest in resettling it again."

"Let me see that for myself," said Tobias, impatient, but Tess snapped the paper away playfully before he could take it.

"I will read it to you," she said, enjoying her power.

"Let me see there—"

"What do you want to know?" asked Tess, looking over the paper. "Around Yuletide, the town is going to have a carnival on the spot where they hanged the witches, and they're going to use the occasion to . . . draw people in."

Horrick nodded. "It's a sad little place, abandoned; people think it's haunted. The New Haven and Boston families who own the town want to rebuild, put all that to rest—"

"Well, that's going to be something of a trick." Tobias snorted.

"Give them a chance; it's just the beginning. It's a nice thing, really. They're rededicating the old town square." Tess read further.

"It's a winter carnival, sort of a celebration—"

"Of having killed witches?"

"Of course not, that was two hundred years ago. Let them bury the past," Tess chastised him. "It's supposed to be a much-needed break in the winter gloom. I would think you above all would appreciate that."

Tobias was thinking, letting her words soak in. "I suppose I do. We could all use a break from the annoyances of the season."

She looked at him, immediately regretful. "Tobias."

"Well, what were you planning to do for Christmas?"

"Something *normal* and traditional. I don't plan to spend the holiday at the reopening of a ghost town. Sooner or later you have to work this ghosthunting business out of your system."

Tobias smiled naughtily, and rested his cello bow on his shoulder. "Sooner or later I will. A few more years of it, and I'm done." She glowered at him, and he said, coaxingly, "Tell me it doesn't sound like fun. The two hundredth year. If I were a ghost witch monstrosity, I'd want to be there."

"That's what bothers me," she said, her humor fading away.

Their mutual sensitivity to the world around them, seen and unseen, was becoming more and more highly attuned. Little things had been bothering her lately, which she hardly admitted even to herself. Now he was confronting it directly. "You don't want to say it, Tess, but you've felt it, too. We're being summoned there. Like a voice in the next room . . . The whole spirit plane is rippling with it. Something is calling us."

"There is always a calling somewhere, if you listen for it. Often it's so faint, it could easily be our imagination."

"Not this time. It's stronger. Piercing. Don't you want to know why?"

Tess grew frightened, and no longer cared to disguise it. "We test fate every time we reach out to a spirit. We're lucky nothing truly regrettable has ever happened to us."

"I want you to consider the outlandish idea that you might someday die a dreadful death, and be left somewhere improper. There you are, and your spirit calls out for help. You are heard by certain sensitives. And ignored. Left to fester unjustly."

His words wounded Tess, who feared loneliness in life, and had never considered such a state in death.

"If you don't wish to join me," Tobias added, "I'll make my own way, and Horrick can look after you."

"Not me, sir," the butler answered. "Your endeavors are too improper for me to continue here. I meant what I said."

Tobias looked back at Tess. She knew Horrick was quite serious; a tremor of disharmony flew out from him, uncertainty about where he would go and what he would do now.

Tobias felt it as well. "Well, Tess, I'm sure you can manage a week or so with just the maids and the cook."

A quiet panic stirred within her at the prospect of losing her first married Christmas with Tobias. He was keenly aware of everything in her heart, as always. She envied his perfect clarity about what he wanted.

Tobias could tell she was leaning toward accepting his offer. "It's simple. A plea is being made. We have to answer this," he said, smiling, his eyes victorious already. "Your curiosity is as awful as mine, you just won't let yourself feel it."

She sighed, making no reply. Tobias took this as agreement.

He looked at Horrick. "When does the train leave for this fine little hamlet?"

And so Christmas plans were made.

CHAPTER FIVE

❧

Not a day later, they took the quickest, most direct way available to them, at least according to Horrick. Tobias was sad to see him go. A butler who knew where to get occult artifacts and make decent travel arrangements was hard to find.

As the small ship from New York to Massachusetts groaned and rocked, Tess stood on deck in the cold air and kept herself from worries of drowning by examining Tobias's behavior instead.

He was inside the ship, enjoying the camaraderie of other travelers, but Tess had needed separation from the group. Crowds were a poison to her. *Quit thinking about it*, she told herself. Quit thinking about what it would be like if the boat were to sink, and what the screaming, panicked passengers would look like, and sound like, and feel like. *I'm trying*, she thought again. Not hard enough.

Then she wanted to laugh. *Normal people have conversations with other people. Stop nurturing these images of your death in a completely unlikely disaster and think of something else.*

Consider Tobias.

Tess felt herself wondering how she had gotten pushed into

this dark journey, with barely a day to prepare. She laid out the meager clues, one by one. *A graveyard spirit tells us that not all the accused in Salem were innocent. Horrick uncovers an unnamed First Accused, a person who may have fled with the others to the mysterious, dead town of Blackthorne, where there is now a winter carnival.* And, though it was too vague to count as evidence, she and Tobias had begun sensing a kind of distress call. Or was it merely the power of suggestion?

She reconsidered. No, it wasn't that alone. There *were* emanations from the woods beyond Salem, and they were strong. To be precise, it felt something like a wave of chilled air, or like hearing a roaring crowd from a great distance.

But Tobias was not above a bit of cunning to convince her to do what he wanted. It occurred to her this was happening more often. These emanations *were* real. So why the trickery, the oiling of the truth? He made that a habit for others, but why now for her?

She wondered if she knew him well enough to say. He was hardly a bully, but he had seemed more concerned with her happiness when she was in Pennsylvania. In his letters back then, he quoted poetry and wrote fantastic meditations on the change of seasons or about birdsong—imagine him reciting pretty little poems now. She couldn't help feeling rather ensnared, caught up in his recklessness.

She remembered a moment when they first met, at the church overrun with orphans, when he had cleverly sent a constantly chattering boy on an errand so that Tess could have some quiet. She had been impressed with his ability to keep the others away and to protect her without seeming overbearing. Later, he had become artful in managing his uncle, who would never do anything Tobias wanted unless Tobias could trick him into it.

But the years with Uncle were just part of the picture. Tobias had always needed to shepherd people carefully. His father and mother had rarely paid attention to him unless he did something outrageous or morbid—so Tobias strived to satisfy them.

His parents had argued frequently, and Tobias learned to lie to each about the other's habits to avoid conflicts.

Thinking about this, Tess arrived at the conclusion life had rewarded Tobias for his minor deceptions. The question was, did he employ his bag of tricks with her? Regardless, she had to admit he was terribly amusing when he wasn't scaring her to death.

The chill wind shifted. The boat was steering toward port. The weak flow of spirit tidings coming from the land seemed to grow slightly, to push against her mind.

Inside the ship's cabin, Tobias felt the prickling in his head, the turning of some faraway spirit force and he lusted for it. He calmed himself by looking out the porthole at the lonely figure of his wife on deck. *What a unique girl she is*, he thought. *With a full mind and heart. Not like the boring, prattling society birdbrains in here. Is it only because I let my wife be as she wishes and other husbands do not?*

"Is she yours?" asked a nearby gentleman, who reeked of jealousy, like a scent on his skin.

"You mean like a horse or a caged bird?" said Tobias. "No. But we've been married almost a year . . . and I'm afraid the constant excitement of my company is wearing her down."

"Constant excitement, huh? You think well of yourself."

"Not at all. I long for a day, hopeless though it may be, when I am as colorless and unremarkable as those around me."

"Ah," said the gentleman, oblivious to the insult.

CHAPTER SIX

The Goodravens spent the night in Salem, awaiting the next day's festivities in Blackthorne. They slept at an inn dripping with fangs of icy ivory. Their dreams were unmemorable, washed in a moodless whiteness, as if winter had found a way to freeze the images in their minds. They were left with a sense that in all the world, they had only each other.

When they awoke they felt a heaviness of movement, a dazed quality, as if they had taken a long afternoon nap and could not shake themselves to full alertness. Each felt as if it were not early dawn at all, but a vague, unmoving time of day that had leaked out of their dreams.

Wind rattled the frosted windows. The sensations they'd felt of invisible forces in the forests beyond the city seemed to withdraw. *We are not here*, the presences seemed to say. *Do not worry yourself.*

As Tess dressed, she wondered if the things she sensed in Blackthorne could be sensing her back, becoming aware of her.

Tobias pretended to be energetic, pulling his clothes on quickly, starting a fire, and packing up for the trip. This morning he had the odd feeling that the Blackthorne presence had a *family* characteristic to it. That is, he felt unmistakably that his own father and mother were the ones calling to him.

He did not mention it to Tess. It was impossible that his parents could have anything to do with the Salem witch trials. They had never been to this place. And yet he had a subtle feeling they were, in fact, out there waiting for him. Intriguing.

Was it possible that a spirit could look inside him and be aware of his memories? Could a spirit imitate a feeling of family? He'd never known this to happen before. But if it wasn't mimicry, then what on earth was his family's connection to witches killed two hundred years ago?

Downstairs, he begged a coffee cup from a fellow traveler so he could avoid the babbling innkeeper, Mrs. Celia Harnow, who could be heard clanging pots in the kitchen, her laugh grating obnoxiously at this early hour.

Back in the room, he made an effort to smile at Tess as he threw open the curtains, but he didn't hold her gaze. He had to be careful, or she'd sense his uneasiness.

Keeping his feelings secret was difficult, but vital. Tess had spent much of her early life with a half-mad mother who lavished her with love and affection—then suddenly took it away and hid in her room for days on end. Tess had been trained to need the crutch of someone beside her; at first, a kindly housemaid, and later her governess. She couldn't have him faltering in his confidence.

He'd have to disguise his mood better, perhaps by playing the cello. He put his mind on a melody, and complimented himself on keeping his worries completely silent.

But in fact, Tess could sense perfectly well he was hiding something.

Later that morning the Goodravens arrived at the train station in a comfortable coach. Salem, its frosty harbor bustling with sea traffic and its streets busy with factory clamor, proved harder to get through than expected, but they would make the train to Blackthorne in plenty of time.

As the horses halted, the couple appreciated the stillness for a moment, not wanting to leave the relative warmth of the coach just yet, or to rush into a new crowd of unknown travelers. Tobias took a breath, and nervously tapped his cello case.

"I think sometimes if we didn't have these, I'd lose you to one of those states of yours," Tess said thoughtfully, running a finger over the shoulder of her own instrument case.

"What state is that?" said Tobias, sad-eyed, with phony good cheer. He started to get out, but Tess took his arm.

"We could stay in here and keep warm a little longer, couldn't we?" She tried to look romantic, even scandalous, but she knew her fear of the journey ahead was quite obvious to him.

"Love to." Tobias smiled with equal amounts of reassurance and roguishness. "But the train will be leaving. You can hide in here—but then you'd miss all the fear and terror and wonder of it all." With a mischievous look, he opened the door, taking her hand.

She stepped outside into a cruel wind, as the coachman unloaded their luggage.

They watched as a tired mother rounded up four little girls. She looked surprised to see their instrument cases. "What's this, something to ward off evil spirits?" she joked.

"I hope not," said Tobias.

"Well, we've got plenty around here," said the mother, nodding toward her little girls, who were chasing one another fiendishly. "It's all very romantic really, isn't it?" added the woman. "A perfect escape from the city."

Do we look as if we need escape? Tess wondered. She had thought they appeared like any happy and typical young couple, but her view of "typical" was perhaps not common. Tobias had a bemused expression; he seemed worn-down, but making-the-best-of-it, pulling his coat tight against the cold, his whitish blond hair a part of winter itself. Tess could see herself from a window reflection, so small beside him, but thoughtful, poised, perhaps even beautiful. Her ample dark hair was tied up, loose strands framing her petite features. Not unappealing, overall. Certainly respectable. And she hid her fears quite well.

As the children passed, casting off joyous fragments of wildness and excitement, Tobias watched with some jealousy. He said, "What would you give to feel like that every day?"

Tess smiled at him. "It's Christmas, Tobias. You should be no different."

But then the father of the little girls crossed into the snowy scene, shoving through the crowd, and it was as if the whole world grew suddenly darker. The man had an evil about him; it came off his body like the odor of death itself.

"Children," he yelled, yanking the arm of the youngest, "get out of the way of these people, before I have to punish you, and believe me, I'll use all the force my arm can give."

Their mother turned away, ashamed, while the man looked gruffly toward Tobias, complaining, "Can't leave 'em at home— we're all going to the ice festival."

Tobias eyed him coldly. "That ought to brighten our spirits."

The crush of people had begun streaming into the frosted gates of the Salem train station.

While the coachman took their baggage to the rear of the special express, Tobias and Tess stood apart from the flow of other passengers.

"Last chance to turn back," Tess murmured.

"Nonsense. We're about to find out if there really are witches up there."

A stooped, elderly conductor ambled past them, pushing to get through the gates. "Make way now, or we'll be running late," he muttered. "A lot of out-of-town folk here, looking for land in Blackthorne. Train's crowded. You may need to sit apart."

Tobias looked down at the trainworker. "Oh, we're never apart."

The old man, walking on, looked at him over his shoulder. "Dangerous to need each other so much. I'm a widower, I can tell you a thing or two about that—"

"And no new lady has snatched you up?" mumbled Tobias, under his breath. "You wonder how that could be possible."

"—you'd better get in. They're boarding now, sir," the old man said, not even listening.

Hiding a smile, Tobias imitated the man's fearsome voice, "They're boarding now . . ."

Tess considered him. "You don't have the right inflection. You have to sound more like you're hiding a human head under your coat."

Tobias tried again, darker, more convincing. "They're booooarding now . . ."

"Much better. The human-head element was right there. Palpable."

"Tobias! Tess!"

Behind them, Celia Harnow, the innkeeper, arrived, her golden curls bouncing as she hurried to them. She was a large, bubbly, blustery woman, whom Tess thought somewhat likable in all her stumbling kindness, though Tobias found her quite annoying, which he openly admitted.

"You forgot your train tickets at the inn!" she said, her baby face flushed.

"Thank you, Mrs. Harnow," Tess said politely.

"I'm so jealous of you two, tighter than two doves. Me, I'm stuck with the old goat. He wants me to stay with the inn and feed him and his firemen friends, so I can't even go to the carnival." The "old goat," her husband, was the usual target of her complaints.

"Yes, thank you, ma'am, we've got to be going now," said Tobias. Moving away from the inkeeper as he whispered to Tess, "The dead hate to wait."

As they neared the line for the train, Tess saw the four little girls again. Nearby, a scowling, thin woman was arguing with a porter over a cart piled with some boxes. "Be careful with those, they have my dolls in them. They're for sale at the festival." She rudely warned one of the girls, "Don't touch these. They're not for you to play with."

Tobias watched the sweet, tiny child turn sad. Out of spite, he reached over and swiped one of the woman's boxes. Tess hid her amusement. As the thin woman fussed, not even noticing him, Tobias broke open the box and pulled out a boy doll. He looked at the girl. "What do you want for Christmas?" he asked.

Tess watched the little girl answer, "Mmm, something . . ."

Tobias grinned, handing her the doll. "Like this?"

"Something scary." The girl giggled.

"Something scary? For Christmas?" Tobias asked.

"She loves scarecrows and Halloween," said the child's sister, while her parents obliviously moved ahead.

"Sounds like my kind of girl." Tobias pulled the head off the doll. "Headless horseman," he said. "All you need is a horse."

"You're a strange man," the girl said.

"Yes," said Tobias, good-naturedly. "Yes, I am."

Tess reached out to squeeze the girl's hand. "Tess Goodraven," she said, and gestured to Tobias. "My husband, Tobias Goodraven."

"Husband?" The girl laughed. "You're too small to be married."

"Not at all." Tess smiled back.

The girl's father turned, calling the children angrily, and Tess could see Tobias growing tense. "What I love about Christmas is, it always brings out the best in people," she joked uneasily.

Tobias took on a mock-scary voice. "And all the ghosts get homesick."

She kissed him. "I feel brave."

They moved toward the train, with its magnificent black engine, dragon-breathing steam over the imposing station, whose square brick towers and buttresslike side wings were ominously reminiscent of a medieval fortress.

Several youngsters turned to Tess, shocking her, for their eyes were pearly white and fixed upon nothing in particular. Others stood with closed eyes, and carried canes to help them along. The blind children stood with their chaperones, and Tess felt a pang of sadness that they could not see the sorcery of winter around them, the beauty that the train and the station created together.

Everyone was silent. Tobias and Tess stood out brilliantly from the crowd; as always, he in gray, she in white. They looked around, observing every detail with amusement and fascination, as the snow collected on the other passengers' drab black and brown coats.

Normal people. Odd little curiosities.

The train was now ready, but the pace of boarding was slow. Impatient, Tobias led Tess away from the others, and entered through a coach farther up, slipping a bribe to a steward.

The train was a masterpiece. Tess and Tobias moved through several parlor cars, beautifully appointed in dark leather and mahogany. The trip today would be a short one, but the festival organizers had spared no expense.

As they walked through the first-class section, car after car grew more opulent. Tess found herself wanting to sink into the chairs of each room, for they were truly rooms, dripping with grandeur, presenting plush sofas, dazzling chandeliers, and wide windows, rooms in which millionaires like J. P. Morgan or Andrew Carnegie would have looked quite at home.

Then came the dining car, ornamented with cherrywood

tables, brass fixtures, silver, linen, and china—a feasting place for kings. The second dining car was less expensive-looking, but only slightly less extravagant.

And there was a smoking car, a mobile gentlemen's club complete with upright grand piano, a harp, pre-Raphaelite paintings, and a high ceiling made of glass so that Tess could see the snowflakes drifting down upon them, like in a fairy tale.

Finally Tobias and Tess reached the elegant passenger cars, and found their seats. Tess had traveled quite a bit in her few short years of life, and this train was as perfect a creation as she had ever seen in New York, London, or Paris.

It was a shame every piece of it seemed to radiate a mournful dread.

CHAPTER SEVEN

꩜

Other travelers arrived, in a wave of perfumes and coffee breath, rustling coats smelling damp from snow, excitement mingling with impatience. The Goodravens watched them quietly, trying to gather the full entertainment value from each. Most of them were elderly, perhaps part of various historical societies, but a group of college men provided some color.

Tess heard one of them, a likable overweight fellow, jokingly say, "Is this ice festival good for meeting girls, or not, Sattler? It's not just pruny old maids with stalactites on their noses, is it?"

His friend, Sattler, was the tallest of them, a lanky, relaxed young man with a blond goatee, who gave the overweight college boy a knock-it-off glance.

Tess had the oddest feeling that they were hiding some kind of lie. She didn't know what it could be. But it left an acrid taste in her mouth, and Tess Goodraven was rarely wrong about such things.

The college boys took their seats, and Tess smiled to see them jostle each other and roughhouse. She sometimes forgot that she and Tobias were young at all; they had lived too much to feel very young, and living like older people, on their parents' money, had made them somewhat old in spirit. She knew Horrick thought of them as naughty children, but he was a crotchety old turnip himself, in her opinion.

In the murmur of conversation, she heard the overweight student, Ned, arguing with Michael, a gloomy, sullen young man, thin, cold, and bespectacled. "It's going to be amazing, it'll be the talk of the music school," Ned said to him.

"You're an idiot," Michael replied.

Ned turned to Tess and Tobias. "Let me ask you something," he said. "Is it or is it not brilliant to take the work of Nietzsche and set it to music for an opera?"

Tess just stared at him.

"Singing it in German," he went on. "Isn't that the smartest thing you've ever heard? Would that not be truly greatness?"

"I don't know," said Tess, amused. "I . . . don't speak German."

Ned was annoyed, but the other student, Michael, seemed satisfied. The train lurched forward, giving Tess a jolt, and Tobias took her hand. "You said you weren't afraid."

She tried to look calm. "You're with me. I'm not afraid."

But she was. She was afraid whenever she stepped out of their New York house, though she took pride in the fact that it never stopped her. She just carried her anxiety with her and rolled it into a ball in her stomach.

From the window, Tess could see Celia the innkeeper outside at her carriage, sadly watching the train depart. From what Tess had observed, Celia was constantly bickering with her coachman. The conversation was easy to imagine:

He would be saying, "It's not my fault you can't go. I'm not your husband."

"He doesn't control me," Celia would say. "I can hop aboard that train any time I want."

"Let me stop it for you," the driver would say caustically. "I'll throw myself in front of it."

And Celia would snipe at him, "You won't get extra pay for it."

"The day I get extra pay . . ."

"Oh, shut your mouth."

Tess smiled at her ideas. She knew she was closer to the truth than not. How awful for Celia to be ordered about by her husband, Tess thought. But it was common. Tess was more concerned about being left behind than chained up; Tobias was too wild, and she wondered sometimes if she could keep hold of him.

In the growing snowfall the train charged away from the Salem station.

As steam blocked her window, Tess looked over their companions in the car. From their spot near the back, she and Tobias could see everyone. The older couple closest to them were named Gil and Elaine. Gil was a relentlessly serious man with a great port-wine mark that stretched across his face from his forehead to below one eye. Tobias whispered that he looked as if his wife had hit him over the head and the blood had stained him permanently. Elaine seemed to be a rather gracious individual, quietly anticipating the celebration to come.

"Getting worse out there, you'd say?" Gil was saying, gazing out the window. He seemed to issue a standard grunt at the end of his remarks.

"I would have rather stayed in," his wife answered, "but it's probably good for me to go. They're doing fireworks at the end of it?"

"Yes. They'll do fireworks. They spent a good deal of money on them."

"Was that one of your recommendations?"

"One of the few things they listened to. The Blackthorne investors were so stupidly impatient, unh? You don't have a winter carnival to draw people to your town. You're supposed to bring them in spring or summer. Make them forget the harsh Decembers."

"You're involved in the carnival?" Tess asked him.

He seemed annoyed by her forwardness. "Yes, I'm a history professor. I study human-migration patterns. The Blackthorne council paid me to figure a way to bring people back to town."

"And what did you tell them?"

"Not to have this carnival. I told them the key ingredient in drawing people to a place is lust."

"Lust?"

"Yes, ma'am. We mustn't shy away from the word, unh? If your land has nothing to offer—far from city and culture, hard and mediocre farming, winters cruel and long—then you use the lure of starting a family. I said to the town elders, 'Give some little bit of property to all the young women you can find, and spread the word in every metropolis that your town has the prettiest unmarried ladies the world's ever seen.' Let nature do the rest.

Learn from P. T. Barnum. Advertise. They just laughed me off. They said modern inventions like telephones and fancy trains were more to their liking. Waste of money, hmm?"

His wife was shaking her head. "He'll tell you more than you want to know. My husband is a man of ideas. How I love him." Elaine laughed.

That was a lie. She hated him and Tess could feel that it no longer even troubled the older woman. It smelled like the lingering stench of rotten fruit.

"My husband is much the same," said a beautiful, cheaply dressed young lady. "An engine of ideas. I can never get enough."

That was a lie as well. The woman thought often of killing him, which left a black stain in the air wherever she went. Tess smiled weakly. The husband, in his twenties, had lean good looks and clearly knew where every strand of his dark hair lay. Tess decided to call these two Mr. and Mrs. Tawdry-Sinful.

The man grinned at Tess with indecent intentions. Then his gaze moved on toward another woman, whose eyes flashed in his direction.

Tobias took all this in with amusement. "Love is everywhere, isn't it?"

Tess looked back at him, but Tobias was hardly bothered by Mr. Tawdry-Sinful's behavior. She began wishing he would be more jealous. Now there was a sense she rarely got from him.

Jealousy was hardly a rare commodity, she mused. Other girls seemed to find Tobias, with his confidence and easy manner, more than a little attractive. And his low, assured voice. Women loved the voice.

The historian might have been right about the power of lust. To the Goodravens, it appeared as heat, and a vivid musky smell. In fact, even as Gil had mentioned it, Tess had noted his wife's interest in several of the younger men on board. It was completely hidden from most, but Tess was bothered by the woman's lack of decorum, even if only in her daydreams.

These kinds of considerations were nothing Tess ever spoke about to anyone but Tobias, because no one would understand her, except perhaps another spiritualist. The vocabulary for describing human feeling was, sadly, too limited. But for Tess and Tobias, after the trauma of the theater fire—and with every spirit encounter since—emotion had become a palpable thing.

It wasn't just that she and Tobias took feelings in from others like a scent or a pressure upon the skin or like sounds or flashes of light, but on top of that, there seemed to be so many more *types* of emotion than was usually understood to exist.

Emotion flowed around them like highly distinct, living things and there were so many sentiments for which there were no words. Tess had many times been witness to the special worry a person had for a missing pet, which manifested as a tingling in her heart. She had also recognized that peculiar disconnection between what some people expressed and what they actually said, as when an impolite woman spoke harshly but continued smiling. This she and Tobias experienced as a low hissing, much like a teakettle before it screams.

One could fill an encyclopedia with these unnamed sentiments. The Salem graveyard experience in particular had been, for an instant at least, a blasting of all the emotions at once as the spirit entered. She understood how Tobias could crave these communions.

The train clacked onward. The interplay with the Tawdrys and Mr. Boring Wine Mark was over, and Tess was left listening to the college crew chattering wildly up ahead.

"—what's the truth of it?" asked Ned. "The festival grounds are supposed to be haunted by Blackthorne's witches—but who *were* these witches?"

Sattler's pretty friend Annette waved away this idea and spoke up for the first time. "If you lived around here," she said, "you'd laugh about it. A silly old legend is what it is. The 'Runaways of the Salem Witch Trials' sounds spooky, but I don't think it ever happened." Tess wasn't sure she liked Annette; she seemed excessively happy and not very bright, like a kitten rolling around a ball of yarn, excitement tumbling out of her. "The only thing I know," the girl added, "is an old nursery rhyme we used to say about one of them . . . 'Old Widow Malgore, dance upon her grave—'"

Others on the train joined in. "—Old Widow Malgore, she keeps a devil slave . . . Old Widow Malgore, your daughter never knew, Old Widow Malgore, the curse you made for two . . ."

The chant began to break up, people forgetting the rest of the ditty, except Annette: "Old Widow Malgore, your devil will break free . . ." as others finally recovered the tune, shouting out, "And vengeance you will see!"

"Well, what does all that mean?" Ned laughed.

Annette shrugged him off. "Oh, I don't know. Ask Michael; he knows more about it, I think."

It seemed to Tess that Annette might be hiding feelings for the serious, bespectacled Michael, but she couldn't be sure. Certainly Sattler, her companion, did not know of any romantic betrayal; he had introduced Annette as his finacée, with no trace of discontent. As for Michael, Tess could see his interest in the girl was obvious and mixed with painful remorse. This Michael was a young man with a conscience, perhaps.

She noticed the wine-marked historian, Gil, looking at his wife, wanting to interrupt the discussion.

But it was Michael who spoke. "After the witch hunts, Blackthorne got wiped out by an epidemic, and no one ever rebuilt 'til now. It became a ghost town. I heard they burned the witches in the old town square, but no one knows the whole story."

"Someone knows." At the very back of the train, a dark, impressively tall man interrupted in a low, accented voice. He wore a wide-brimmed hat that concealed his face, and his figure blended with the darkness, where the window shades had been drawn against the glare from the snow.

Tess expected him to educate them, but instead he turned his head, by way of introduction, toward an older gentleman, who had a long cascade of gray hair and piercing eyes. He looked frail and skeletal, resembling a mummy.

"This fellow here knows," said the foreign-sounding man. "As we were waiting for the train, he told me some things that may concern you. . . ."

His tone worried Tess. The Mummy and the Giant, that's what the two men looked like. She shivered, not least because the older man's gaze had fallen to her and was sending out great tides of fear and anxiety, an awareness that something awful awaited Tess and all the others as well. No, it was more than awareness. It was a *surety*.

CHAPTER EIGHT

W hile the tall foreigner eased back into the shadows, everyone's interest turned to the elderly man, who introduced himself as Josiah Jurey. He smiled, but his grin seemed forced.

Michael smiled back at Jurey, humoring him. "So, then, are you an expert in folk legends and ghost stories?"

"Folktale, you say? A little bit of progress comes in, and the truth becomes a folktale," Jurey replied, dismissing all things youthful and ignorant. "There were three of them. Came up here to escape the witch trials in Salem. They were followed, hunted down, and killed. But they were hanged. Not burned."

The foreigner who sat nearby seemed to enjoy seeing the college boy set straight. It was hard to tell in the dim light, but his head tilted toward Michael as if scolding him.

"The truth is, it's something of a Romeo and Juliet story . . . ," Jurey added.

"Well," prompted Tess, "everyone loves a romance."

"Everyone loves a tragedy," said Tobias.

Jurey, licking his thin lips, needed little encouragement to tell the tale. "There was a young man, Wilhelm, who was seeing a girl named Abigail, back in Salem. And her mother, she hated the boy. It was a fierce hatred. She believed the boy had killed her husband when they were clearing old growth on his land. A falling tree had pinned him down, and the man was crushed to death before help could arrive. But the mother believed it was murder. You see, the father had disliked this boy to begin with. No one was good enough for his daughter.

"Not long after the father died, others died mysteriously, and the witch-hunting began; and Wilhelm and Abigail joined with the whole town to watch the hangings, never knowing they'd be enmeshed in it." His grim voice with its New England lilt was entrancing. "One way or another, mother, daughter, and suitor all ended up in Blackthorne. They were tracked down and killed, all three, accused of witchcraft: the young man, Wilhelm, for consorting with witches and the girl, for the darkest of magics. The crowd, they forced her to kiss the lips of the dead Wilhelm, before she died herself. It is a known fact. And what they say is . . . well . . . in dying these witches somehow left a curse on every person who ever sets foot on this ground to die and be tortured after death, with such brutality that the very soul itself bleeds away."

No one took a breath.

"Or some such," said Jurey, with a touch of pleasure.

The mention of a doomed couple in 1600s Salem gave Tess a slightly unwanted thrill—a delicate disturbance not easily explained by the fact these two had also been reckless and young.

The tawdry man reacted unkindly. "Sir, you seem to have an

unhealthy interest in—"

"Then came the deaths," added Jurey. "Murders. Infants dying in their beds. Suicides. An epidemic came through Blackthorne and wiped everyone out."

"Well, that's quite a lot of death," said Tess. "A curse is almost convincing, I'd say."

"Why? Because there was some sickness? An epidemic, unh?" Gil, the historian, looked at her with contempt. "It's now believed it was cholera, which even today kills people the world over—the devil's work, maybe, but we don't say it's witchcraft. We're smarter than that. The people in Blackthorne let superstition get the best of them, and it drove them to insanity, unh?"

"But people around here believed in the curse, didn't they?" said Jurey. "The town died out. No one ever went back in to live there."

"So many terrible things happened there. Why go back now?" Tess wondered.

"The railroad's built new lines between Salem and Vermont, and they want a shortcut to them," Gil's wife, Elaine, answered her. "That takes 'em right through here. Someone decided to have the winter carnival in Blackthorne to try to bring people back in. The old men of Boston and New Haven who own the town need new blood—young people like yourself—coming here to settle. They can't have this great ugly hole between townships. . . ."

Gil scowled. "You ask me, they ought to cover up the history, the traditions, any trace of the whole thing. You can put a pretty bow around it, but people don't like this 'witching' talk. They're superstitious. Part of old Salem even changed its name to Danvers."

He looked around the car. "Fact is, there are people on this train who are related to those that killed the witches. They don't want that blood on their hands."

Some passengers did indeed look disturbed.

"We're going into the last piece of America where the Salem witch trials are still a fresh scent in the air," Gil went on. "Folks here remember it well. But history is finally blowing it all away. They're even going to put in electricity up there. Scare away the spooks." His joke failed, and Gil retreated. "Oh, calm yourselves. Now, just because the town slaughtered a few witches and then was wiped out by a plague doesn't mean there's a curse on it."

Everyone stared at him in dead silence. Tess wanted to laugh.

"Well, it's an *adorable* story," said Tobias. "I think you should use that to attract people. I mean, there are all kinds of nutty fudges who would love to see where they killed the witches. You should make it the theme of the carnival. Nothing says Christmas to me better than the skeletons of real-life witches, I can tell you that."

As usual with Tobias's remarks, no one was quite sure what he meant at first.

"You should roll out all their old, wormy remains and let us have a look," he continued. "I've yet to see the person who doesn't enjoy seeing a shrunken head or a good hanging, and there's always a big turnout at any funeral wake with an open casket. If you really want people to come to your festival, you've got to get those bodies out and let people get their pictures taken with the witchy cadavers. Dig them up. Someone must know where they are, don't you think?"

Everyone gaped at him. Tess smiled at them broadly.

They were off to a wonderful start with these people.

The train headed into a curve, affording a view of a big ice-coated wooden archway up ahead, with a playfully carved witch's face upon it. WELCOME had been written on an ice slab nearby. Everyone seemed disturbed at the sight of the witch's image at that particular moment.

"Fact of the matter is," added Tobias, "that's why we're here."

"What's why?" asked Gil.

"Well, the ghosts, of course. There's talk that those witches didn't pass on quietly. They're still up there."

Tess added, "We've been all over the world searching for spirit habitations. Who would've thought there was an authentic one right here in New England? I'm positively embarrassed we didn't know about it before."

Tobias looked at her sympathetically. "You can't know about all of them, dearest."

Everyone in the car was now staring at them.

"This habitation could be as good as the one in Switzerland," she said.

"Don't get your hopes up, sweetie," Tobias replied. "It could be a hoax. You come all the way out, you pay your money, and what is it? Nothing but flashing lights and hokum." He paused. "Of course, flashing lights have their appeal. . . ."

A dour-faced, prudish woman looked at Tess with some disgust. "You really seek out ghosts?"

"Dear lady," said Tess, "nothing gives a rush of blood to the body like a good spirit possession. You feel it right down to your intimates. It's a thrill you will not soon forget."

The prudish woman looked shocked. "You've done this sort of thing in the past? Why?"

"Well, I don't want to disturb you by calling it an addiction," Tobias interjected, "but let's just say, you've never really lived until you've been tickled from the *inside*."

Tess and Tobias smiled sweetly.

It was so easy to shock people these days, it almost wasn't fun. Still, there were some passengers who were not bothered at all by talk of death and phantoms. Tess felt the steady gaze of the dark foreigner fall upon her.

"I fear no ghosts," he said, "nor anything else." The man—was he Italian? Spanish?—was leaning forward just a bit, into the window light, opening his coat so Tess and everyone else could see he was armed, pistols glinting silver against his dark clothes. "I've been hired by some of these rich old men who own the town. I'm here to make certain there is nothing to fear, neither among rowdy men drunk on spirits nor among spirits who wish to drink the blood of men." He gave a stern smile, and Tess could see the edge of a handsome but unshaven jaw beneath his square Western hat.

"I shall do my best not to fear any dead witches," she said to him.

Tobias looked at the foreigner. "Is there a reason you above any other would be hired for this protection?"

"I have been here and there. Seen the West. Seen blood. Seen death. Seen guns."

"All in one place, or one at a time?"

The foreigner was unamused. "You speak like one who has never seen a fight."

"True enough, I suppose," said Tobias. "But I have other strengths. I have seen the unseeable. How about you, sir? Were you lucky enough to have encountered the supernatural in your journeys?"

"I will say this: I've made up my mind that I won't judge other's beliefs. There's nothing certain, except that God favors the strong. I go where there's money. Witches or not, I come prepared to kill what needs to be killed—"

"There *are* witches in these woods," Josiah Jurey interrupted. "And they are to be respected."

Tobias looked at him with a touch of surprise.

In the moving light, Jurey looked tremendously old, with rivers of wrinkles on his face. "I've hunted their kind in a thousand corners. What you have here has dug itself in and drawn power from a sacrosanct place, forbidden and frightening even to the Indians, long before we came. Those who draw from the wellspring in this darkness will not leave easily. They will be strong. The two hundred-year mark of their death will grant them new vitality. They will travel on demons, with blood in their wake. . . ."

CHAPTER NINE

Mr. Josiah Jurey's tale of living, breathing witches feeding off some eternal power in the wilderness strained even Tess's and Tobias's credulity. The man claimed the Widow Malgore—whom he called "The Wretch"—was likely to be surviving on demon's blood, walking about, free as you please. He went on to say the other accused, Abigail and Wilhelm, might have shared a similar fate.

"After two hundred years, they're alive," Tobias said, feigning seriousness. "How interesting. Are you here on a hunting expedition?"

"I have been drawn here. And my work is of a personal nature," said the old man.

"Ah, a mission of vengeance? One of these things killed your child, perhaps? Killed your wife?"

"One such creature was my wife," said Jurey. "She killed my child."

At his words, a chill ran through the car.

"There will be danger ahead," said Jurey. "And you will all have a part to play."

"Madness," murmured Gil.

"It is always madness that brings true insight," said the foreigner.

Tobias suppressed a laugh. "Do we pay extra for these wisdom . . . nuggets?"

The foreigner leaned forward and gave him an icy stare. "I will protect even you," he said.

Annette smiled nervously. "Gunmen, witchhunters," she said. "Didn't anyone come for ice-skating and sleigh rides? This is to be a carnival, after all."

Mr. Tawdry broke in: "We heard of this at a séance in Connecticut. Sounded like a thrill."

His wife smiled. "Our macabre curiosity rears its head."

It had begun to seem that quite a few of the travelers would be more than happy to see the dead witches come to life. Tess felt herself in wilder company than she at first thought. She began to see how these ordinary people were in many ways hoping for something dreadful to happen—to someone else.

"A-sleighing we will go . . . ," sang the foreigner strangely, his eyes on Tobias in an odd challenge. *Have you the strength to face this?* he seemed to say.

Still, Annette and many of the others looked perturbed, as if unhappy to see the kind of people they were traveling with. It would seem a few had indeed come for mere sleigh rides and fireworks.

Outside, the snow-shrouded woods were silent, ominous. Lifeless. Not even a rabbit disturbed the ground. All the usual wildlife had fled. The train thundered past, a long black scar blowing ivory steam through the relentless snowfall.

The old town pulled the train closer.

Some people still sent Tess and Tobias curious and rude glances, but the train had all but returned to normal. Sattler and Annette were laughing quietly. Tess and Tobias watched them, seeing their own behavior mirrored somehow more gracefully in the way the two lightly enjoyed each other's company. Perhaps Tess had been wrong in thinking Annette could be unfaithful.

Feeling their stares, Sattler looked over, seeming perturbed by what he imagined was Tobias's interest in Annette. Then Sattler noticed the Goodravens' cello cases. "What's in there?"

"Cello," said Tobias.

"Both of you play?"

Tobias nodded.

Sattler paused. "You aren't going to play at the carnival, are you?"

"I never leave my instrument. It soothes my nerves. We aren't playing for money, if that's what you mean," said Tobias.

"Good. I thought you were competition. Michael does sketches. We were going to try to earn a bit."

Tobias regarded him. "He draws portraits? Is he any good?"

"He's awful. But we have the whole thing worked out quite well. See, we show this sketch of me . . ." Sattler pulled out a drawing pad.

Tobias looked. "That's fairly nice."

"Yes, we had this fellow back home do it. What we do is, I pretend as if I bought this drawing from Michael, and then hopefully he gets another customer to step up and get a portrait done."

"I don't understand. If he can't draw, what happens when they see *his* work?"

Sattler smiled at Tobias, letting him in on the secret. "He never finishes. He pretends to take a long time finding inspiration, then he starts sketching, and it just goes on and on and on. He makes it take forever, and the customer always decides to get his money back. But then Michael acts offended, and he usually ends up getting half the asking price."

"You annoy these people to death. For profit."

"Pretty much, yes."

"This has worked for you before?"

"It's getting us through college."

Tobias couldn't help but grin. Sattler smiled back.

"Beware the art student with no money," Michael added gloomily.

Well, Tobias had found some complex personalities to amuse him. Tess, fishing about for a passenger of similar value, looked toward Annette. "How about you? Are you interested in the arts as well?"

"Oh, I understand little of the arts," Annette replied energetically. "I've decorated my father's inn where I work, and that's the extent of it. But I have an idea that the arts could be used to help children learn about the world and history and all that."

"Really?"

"I've been thinking I might help the blind students from Salem. You know, they have so little. They're relocating their school up here because they've been given a cheaper arrangement for land. All those rich Boston investors rebuilding Blackthorne were so kind to them, once those children stood right in front of them as a choir, singing hymns. Anyway, I'd like to do my part by teaching them to paint."

"Teaching blind children . . . to paint." Tess strained to imagine it. "What fascinating work they would produce. But you yourself don't know how to paint?"

"Oh, no, not at all."

"Ah."

Tess stared out the window. Strange, wispy whorls of snow spun out of the forest. The train's huffing and clacking drowned out other sounds, but the world outside seemed caged; the wind was like an eager animal wanting escape, straining to be unleashed. The sky was cream and gray, preparing to storm, a pale tiger lying in wait.

From every window Tess could see white-capped trees sheltering nothing but darkness. She had the impression the train was now breaking through a membrane into a place out of time, not just a void between townships, as Elaine had suggested, but a long, solitary kingdom of loneliness.

A deathscape.

In its mind's eye, the creature watched as the train approached a bend near a frozen lake, a vast sheet of ice, and it observed an unnatural heat wave that penetrated the air, and then vanished. It was as if the locomotive were wrapped in a glistening, invisible curtain, and then suddenly this wave shot away from the train into the trees, too quickly to be noticed.

In the distance was a huge herd of elk, rattled, agitated.

The wretch was witnessing these events from a considerable distance, examining the situation, seeing all the elements at work.

Its hand was clawing at the water in a small, smoldering pit built into the floor of a ramshackle house. The pit was encircled by bones, human spines linked together. The skull of a dead elk floated up from the turgid water.

Far off in the forest the locomotive approached the herd of elk.

Tobias put his hand to his temple in excruciating pain. A moment later Tess felt it, too. She looked out the window again. At first she saw only a colossal sheet of glass, a bright *nothingness* surrounded by trees. It shocked her; a white hole in the world. But it was just the blinding gleam of the frozen lake.

As Tess took this in, she became aware of something under the rattle of the train; the sound of something big moving in the woods.

A gentle mist embraced the locomotive, passing, leaving beads of moisture on the window glass. Tess reached out her hand to the window closest to her. *Warm* . . . As she took her hand away, she could see a herd of elk galloping alongside the train. Their hooves on the ground made a powerful drumming.

It caught her completely by surprise.

They had emerged from the forest across from the icy lake. The herd was now a single force of nature, moving nearby as the express chattered on.

The hordes of elk thundered closer.

They were keeping pace with the train.

People beside Tess turned, taking note in awe—the blur and clatter of the herd silencing everyone. The elk were racing the train, the huge, dangerous animal mass smashing across the snow. It was a mesmerizing sight.

For a split second, a shimmer seemed to pass over the elk, as if they were a mirage, and a momentary crackling phenomenon played upon their antlers like lightning. Then the creatures suddenly rushed into the path of the engine.

They dashed across the rails in a throng. The engineer screamed. The first elk intersected with the front of the train, and the engine plowed into them—cutting the huge stampede with a horrific clatter of horns and the thump of raw meat. Elk were hurtled, flying into the air, the cluster of animals shotgunned apart by the cowcatcher, as the train reached a segment of battered, loosened rails.

With a shower of sparks, the train lost its hold on the track.

The old engine slipped sideways, derailed, plowing into the snowbank.

Tess closed her eyes as Tobias threw himself over her.

The engine smashed into the snowy earth.

And the world went dark for everyone.

When Tobias awoke in the upturned train, Tess was nowhere to be found.

CHAPTER TEN

Tobias pulled himself out of a gaping hole in the side of the car. From the corner of his eye, he saw wisps of light shoot off into the forest away from the wreckage. Dizzy, in a daze, his heart beating in panic, he crawled away from the half-destroyed express coach, searching for Tess.

He could see her lying in the snow up ahead. He ran to her quickly, turning her over. She seemed unhurt, with only a few scratches. She looked up, numb.

"Something dragged me," she said.

They turned back to the trench behind her in the snow. Her body had indeed been dragged from the train.

She'd been pulled out of the car.

There was nothing else around her to indicate what had done this, no foot tracks or odd markings.

Unnerved, Tobias looked out across the winter landscape.

Elk corpses lay everywhere. One fearful elk that had survived clattered past to join a few others, which fled across the frozen lake. Human bodies and debris were strewn across the snowbank. The locomotive engine itself lay far ahead in the snow, and the first cars of the train were thrown about behind it.

To both Tess and Tobias, the universe seemed muted, stoppered up. They just stared for a moment, their breath ghosting the air. The middle cars, including theirs, were off the track but near it, some still linked up, and the last part of the train, unhooked from the rest, remained on the rails and intact.

The Goodravens got to their feet, facing the train and the jumble of three derailed cars nearby. Where they stood now was a blank slate of snow; behind them, a dense, winter-dead forest. Across from them, and across the train tracks, there was the frozen lake, and then more trees. Some of the train had slipped from the rails in that direction; thus there were derailed cars on both sides of the tracks.

Most of the massacred elk lay spread around the front of the engine, though some of the corpses curved around Tess and Tobias in a wide, bizarre crescent of brown and blood red.

"God . . . what were these animals doing here?" whispered Tobias. Elk in the northeast were a decidedly rare sight, though pockets of them were seen occasionally. Still, this was not natural. And . . .

"Do you hear that?" whispered Tess. "Those are dead screams."

Tobias nodded. The sound of the freshly dead left a peculiar ringing hum, but never had they heard it so powerfully. "They'll trail off in a while. Just . . . stay calm, Tess."

Other passengers began emerging from their car. A few who had been thrown onto the snow began to stir, waking.

"I think we're good and sound," Tobias said. "Nothing broken?"

"No," said Tess, but she felt herself filling up with nausea and confusion. "I think I've got to get out of here. It's too much . . ."

"Tess. It's going to be all right." He looked over at the wreckage, took in a lungful of cold air. "We're going to understand this."

Though he was rattled, he sounded firm, and his voice steadied Tess. He looked again at the trail in the snow, and then at the train. Curious, intent, he began moving toward the train. She watched him make his way back to the coach, where the college boy, Sattler, seeming shocked and mystified, was sitting on the car that had been turned upon its side. Blood was caked on his blond hair.

Tobias said nothing to him, his mind fixed on some urgent mystery.

Sattler looked toward him. "There are people moving in there," he said slowly, peering down into the car. "We should get them out."

"I suppose someone should," said Tobias. Tess could just hear them. She watched as Tobias climbed onto the coach.

As Tobias looked down, all he could see was a mess of people and metal. Sattler stood blankly beside him. It was a daunting sight, and neither had any idea where to start.

"Should we just pull them out?" asked Sattler. "Maybe that's not good . . ."

Inside the car, the historian, Gil, was helping his wife, Elaine. He looked up, confused but not injured. "The train came off the tracks . . . ," he said to them.

"Indeed it did," said Tobias, grim and unruffled.

Sattler was biting his lip, clearly upset. "I think maybe we should move them, unless they're trapped. We have to keep them warm while we wait for help."

Tobias nodded. "Any way to *get* help?"

"I'm not really sure."

Below them, Tess turned. She could hear other survivors now. Everywhere, out on the snow, in the train cars. Moaning. Screams.

She looked over at Tobias, but he was preoccupied, slapping Sattler's back. "Well, you head up the rescue; you seem to be an upstanding gent," Tobias was saying, moving to examine the metal hole, the torn steel of the roof.

"What are you doing?" Sattler asked him, angered by his giving orders.

"I'm going to be busy for a moment. You find that . . . indeterminately foreign fellow, he'll help you. . . ."

But the foreigner was out already, on the ground, emerging from the car's rear door, carrying an injured Josiah Jurey on his back. Tess looked over at the foreign man and realized this was the first time she'd had a good look at him. She couldn't tell how old he was, but he was unusually tall, sharp and striking-looking, with features she decided were Italian, and he wore a long duster coat and black boots. He had the swagger and air of an elegant outlaw, and, as he threw off his coat, it was clear he had a greatly overdeveloped physique. He was almost monstrously big, but Tess confessed to herself he looked somewhat heroic. It was rather a comfort to know he was there.

The Giant and the Skeleton, as she called them, had survived for the moment. The foreigner set Josiah Jurey down on the snow nearby, holding his head up. Jurey was hurt badly, perhaps mortally, but his alert eyes were on the woods. "Is witchcraft done this."

"Sir?" Tess watched the old-timer curiously.

"There shall be a time of renewal for them. We should strike now. While their energy is spent."

Tess looked up at Tobias, who shook his head, shouting down to the large man, "Sir, can you leave him for a moment? I see here . . . many other people who need help."

"This must be done first," said Jurey, and he pulled the giant closer. Tess watched as the foreigner listened and nodded, and took from the old man a fistful of crosses and necklaces, amulets of some kind, which he pocketed. Then Jurey gave him something else, but Tess couldn't see what it was. She was not entirely sure if the other man was taking Jurey seriously, but he seemed to accept each item solemnly. Then, as Josiah Jurey lost his last strength and closed his eyes, the foreigner eased him down and pressed one of the crosses into the old traveler's hand.

Immediately, the foreigner pulled from his belt a long pistol (one of many), and loaded it. He headed past Tess, off toward the woods, away from the wreckage.

Tobias stood on the train and watched the tower of a man striding away. "What does he think he's . . ." He shouted to the foreigner: "We have need of you here. Sir? Sir!"

"Wilder," the man said without turning back.

Tobias was aggravated. "Wilder? That's your name?"

"It's the name I've taken." The foreigner continued on, as several injured people moaned for help near his path. He would not be taken off course. Whatever Jurey had told him to do, Wilder took it as a life-or-death matter. He was fast disappearing into the woods.

"That man is mad," Tobias complained. "Bring some people over to assist us, Tess, quick as you can."

As Tess stumbled past Jurey's thin body, his eyes suddenly opened. In shock, she stared down at his white face and gaping mouth, as his breath poured out of him and shrouded him like smoke.

"Child," he whispered. "Whatever it is that gives you strength, they will take it from you. Don't give it up. Find anything that gives *them* strength . . . and seize it."

His slackening breath took away the remainder of his words. His dead eyes unleashed a tear that froze upon his face, and Tess hurried away, not looking back, wading through the snow toward the next car.

Her voice shook as she cried out, "Does anyone know of a way to call for help?"

The plea was picked up; she heard people shouting it everywhere. No one knew how to get help quickly, and Tess was beginning to feel ill from the ocean of fear and worry all about her.

She knew Tobias would sense the emotions just as strongly. Their empathic tendencies, as he often called them, seemed louder, deeper, clearer here in the woods. Tess felt overwhelmed by the bursting, sorrowful passion of so many wounded. And it was the fright she sensed—shrill, icy, coming in flashes of blue light—more than any pain, that threatened her most.

She heard a voice from inside one of the cars, a male voice. *"We have too much blood in here. . . . Help me . . . Help me . . ."*

Unable to trace the sound, Tess yelled in desperation, "DOES ANYONE KNOW THE NEAREST HOUSE?"

There was no immediate answer, and Tess wandered toward another train car ahead, to be confronted by its horrors. At first in the shifting light of the snowfall, she could make out only arms and legs through the window, and she couldn't make sense of what she was seeing . . . then amid the moving flesh she saw a man clawing his way over the pile of bodies, pulling himself out through a smashed window.

Tess felt her heart shudder—the man had no legs; they were shorn off below the knee, but they were not bloody, as though burned off, cauterized. He crawled up, automatic, inhuman, clambering over people—

Tess watched in shock as the legless man emerged—reaching out his hand to her, desperate.

She couldn't move. He pulled himself out, his ragged legs thrashing, as he tumbled atop her onto the snowy ground.

He was pressing her down into the cold. He writhed, grunting, a mass of flesh and fear. She struggled, but he was heavy, and seemed to have no sense of what he was doing. His whole body was shuddering uncontrollably, and she felt as if she had hold of an immense fish that was losing strength with every moment in the air. The motion of her hand brushed past his severed limb, and then she grasped snow, trying to pull herself away. She thought she might be covered in his blood, but there was no blood. And then suddenly the bottom of his legs were there now—where jagged, useless stumps were a minute ago. Tess stared at him in horror. He couldn't seem to believe it himself, his eyes stretched wide. She couldn't speak.

He collapsed in the snow.

She untangled herself and pulled free of him. She was in shock, she told herself, and shock leads to hysterical visions. *Calm, now. Calm. Calm.*

CHAPTER ELEVEN

Inside the first ruined train car, Tobias was trying to find his seat. He sidestepped Sattler, who was helping several people out. Tobias raised his voice. "Those of you in here, listen. If you're able-bodied"—he looked doubtfully at old Gil—"then help other people to get out. There may be a risk of fire now. We have one simple mission: survive until help comes. We can do that, can't we?"

Sattler was helping Annette. "Get my satchel over there," he told her. "We might need those things."

Sattler's concern for his bag caused Tobias to worry for his own beloved cello. As soon as the passengers were cleared out, he'd have to search for the instrument cases amid all the tossed-about baggage.

In the meantime, Tobias ran his hand along the jagged metal and shards of glass that were stuck in his seat, all of which had narrowly missed him. It looked as if something had shielded him from the blows, and the debris had rained off in all directions around him. Remarkable, he thought. So it wasn't Tess alone that had been helped to survive. But *why*? His mind stayed on this puzzle, until he finally realized the need around him, jostled by

Michael and Ned, who were assisting people off the train.

Both had dazed expressions seeming to ask for guidance. "We need more help," Tobias said. "Is there telephone service somewhere out here? Blackthorne boasts how modern it is; it seems possible . . ."

Gil looked at Sattler. "Didn't a doctor move back in the woods near here? He wanted them to bring the telephone lines along to his house, didn't he?"

"I'm not sure. I've been away at Harvard," said Sattler. "I don't know the area well . . ."

"We should start asking people," said Tobias.

"I'll see to that."

Gil stopped Sattler. "We should also start some fires for warmth. Have all these boys go and help whoever they can, get blankets, and so on."

Bruised and battered, the college boys strode toward other passengers on the snowfield. They passed Tess, who was moving away from the unconscious man, as a train conductor stumbled around a car.

"Go," he said, and Tess realized he had a leg injury. "Go, get to the engine car. They may have an emergency box, medicines . . ."

Urged on by him, Tess went toward the engine, a black mass against the ivory landscape. It was a long walk, and the sounds of pain filled the air behind her.

An engineer lay up ahead, apparently dead, thrown from the engine cabin. She approached and could see the engineer's body had leaked blood into the snow, a pool of it now *slowly being sucked back into his body.*

She stopped, staring, unsure this had actually happened.

"Oh God . . . help me . . ." Her words escaped in a whisper, and she looked back for help. Instead she discovered the legless man behind her had vanished from the snow, and only the crush of ice where he lay remained as evidence he'd ever been there. People were too busy to take note, or to see her at all. The only one to look over was the conductor who'd sent her forward, now collapsed and in pain. He yelled impatiently, "We've got no way to signal anyone, we need supplies—is there anything in there?"

Trembling, Tess moved closer to the locomotive, confused, hating every step she had to take. Inside the engine cab, a trainworker lay dead, his eyes open and fishlike. There was a strange mist about him, possibly steam, and Tess fumbled around to find anything useful when she was suddenly startled.

The dead man had moved.

She saw his reflection in a brass fitting in the engine cabin. His bloated, watery eyes had fixed upon her.

She kept herself very still.

"Tess . . . ," the worker hissed out of unmoving lips.

For an instant, she tried to ignore it, forcing herself to recognize the sound as being from her imagination, but the hiss came again, quieter. "Tess . . ."

She turned in horror—stifling a scream—but the body was still. She stared at it, shaking, wondering if she'd conceived it out of true distress. But she knew she hadn't.

Bodies could do things they weren't supposed to do. She and

Tobias had heard of at least half a dozen places on Earth where a body could move after death, sometimes long after death, if the elements were right. She had read of it many times, but to see it happen with her own eyes was more disturbing than she could have imagined.

She emerged from the engine, terrified, and empty-handed. She needed Tobias, just for a moment, to settle her mind.

Up ahead, helping passengers out of a car, Tobias yelled to her, "Did you see something? Was anything in there?"

She couldn't answer. He could see her fear, but he couldn't come to her.

Trying to control her mind, she walked back down the tracks toward him, her boots crunching through the snow. Sattler and the other young men walked the snowfield to her left, assisting the injured. Two other gentlemen, strong men who looked to be in their forties, pulled open a banged-up train door.

Tess saw the first man signal Sattler. "A lot of these people are in a state of shock and immobility. They're the first-order cases," he told him.

"Where do we get blankets?" said Sattler.

"Believe they've got 'em in the last car."

Sattler, Michael, and Ned headed for the intact caboose, still on the rails.

Tess continued toward Tobias, who was helping the dour, thin woman with the dolls get out of the train car.

"My dolls . . . ," she said. "You have to get them."

Tobias stared at her demurely. "We have more important concerns right now. Like you."

The thin woman stepped awkwardly, and Tobias's hand slipped from her back to below her waist. "Be careful with me," she snapped. "You will not touch me in my . . . unmentionables."

"Madam, everything about you is unmentionable," Tobias muttered under his breath. "Come, come, move along."

Trying to help, he nearly lifted her off the ground. Tess saw the thin woman's surprise, but she knew that despite his lean frame, Tobias had a fullness in his arms. Tess had need of that strength now, but as she tried to get his attention, he moved on and began helping another female traveler from the car.

The lady looked at him, dazed. "I heard . . . There were voices in my head . . . Such cruel voices . . ."

Tobias was intrigued, but nearby in the snow, the thin woman motioned angrily for him to steady her. "I'm not well. This is revolting."

Annoyed at the distraction, Tobias said, "Very useful observation." The gaunt woman glared at him. His hands full with the dazed passenger, he added, "Honestly, can you not see that people are upset? Why don't you help this person?"

He quickly handed off to the doll seller the lady he was assisting.

"Tobias," Tess said, keeping her voice measured. "There's something very wrong . . ."

"Most of the trainworkers are dead, aren't they?" Tobias guessed. "We need to get more help right away."

"It's blood. The blood . . ."

"Tess, you're in shock—"

"No, listen to me—I felt something—"

"Try to find a blanket. Keep yourself warm," Tobias told her, his attention drawn to something between the railcars, a piece of the puzzle that had formed in his mind. He went off to have a look, making quick tracks in the snow.

"Tobias, if you could just wait . . ." She couldn't make her voice *hold* him; somehow, she couldn't sound firm. He had moved away, not far, but just out of reach in every way.

CHAPTER TWELVE

ess just stood there, feeling abandoned, the first time she'd ever felt that emotion with him. They were too close for this to happen.

Tobias, however, was relying on that closeness. Knowing she was with him, he wasted no time on sentiment, instead pondering what lay before him.

Between the cars he could see the rails had bent strangely, pushed out and disconnected from the ties, especially up by the engine. He turned over in his mind the possibility that the elk herd had dislodged the weak rails. But it seemed this was deliberate work, and it occurred to him the approaching elk would have supplied a substantial diversion, so no one aboard would have even noted the problem with the tracks. At the same time, the train would have been accelerating to avoid collision, worsening the effects of the crash.

Behind him, at the caboose, Sattler shouted, "WE'VE FOUND BLANKETS BACK HERE—"

Ned added, "There's a medical supply kit as well. Help us get these things loose from here."

Tobias reluctantly headed over to help them.

Tess reached for his arm. "I need to speak to you."

Tobias didn't look back, and her hand fell against nothing. "I know that, I know, just wait— Go ask where the doctor's house is," he said. "We need to get help quickly."

Tess stood there, stunned.

At the caboose, Ned and Michael were pulling out blankets, as Annette and Sattler opened a medical box. Michael kept shooting glances at Annette, wanting some recognition, but she seemed to avoid his gaze.

Sattler ran his hand through his hair and looked over the supplies without much hope. "I don't think anyone's opened this for years. I guess the morphine would be all right . . ."

Annette glanced at him sharply. "Well, you're the medical student, can't you do something with it?"

Tobias heard him reply quietly, "Don't tell anyone that. I'm afraid I might do more damage than good." Tobias pretended not to hear, and helped unload blankets.

Standing in the snow, Tess wondered how Tobias could not have felt what she had. How had he failed to detect the presences here, the weight of spirit all around them? The wounded conductor came up alongside her, limping, and she fumbled to find words. "Sir, do you know where the doctor's house is? Is it near?"

The conductor was in a daze. He mumbled to her, "I think . . . the old house. Mordecai place."

"I don't understand . . ."

"The house is but five-minutes' walk, if that. Straight up the tree line."

Tess moved toward the woods, prepared to go it alone. She hadn't gone far before a sense of something silent and evil in the forest caught her, and she stared ahead, unable to go farther. There was a deeper darkness in the trees ahead, a pool of emptiness.

She shouted back to Tobias, but he looked irritated. "Go on— you can do this thing, Tess."

Resolved and angry, she yelled back at him, "Tobias Goodraven. You got me out here, you *will* go with me."

Reluctant, he looked at the injured travelers, but moved toward her.

Crossing the snow quickly to meet him, Tess told him everything in a rush, thankful to get it all out. "Listen to me. I'm not in hysterics. Something is out here. There was a wounded man, his blood vanished *inside* him and what I saw . . . Oh God, I don't know what I saw, Tobias . . ."

"Spirits," said Tobias. "A person rejects their own death, they distort the world around them. You know this, Tess—these were untimely deaths. We can expect to see more of it. . . ."

"This isn't like the literature. This isn't a séance with sliding objects on a table or whispers in a dark room." She protested angrily. "This is enormous power. I'm not sure even a witch could master this."

"Let's have no talk of witchery until we are certain what is truly unfolding," argued Tobias, though his low voice wavered in tone. "Don't frighten yourself needlessly. We are educated in this regard, and our knowledge will see us through."

But the sense is so much stronger than before. Perhaps he was covering his feelings to avoid upsetting her. She wasn't mad; it wasn't mere suggestion that had caused her to see things. It wasn't likely that encounters with the dead could suddenly *cause* madness, was it? Was this part of the curse upon this land? *Those who seek the truth in the blood of Salem dead will know nothing but torment in their head. . . .*

Forget those words, she thought. *It's impossible.*

Tobias seemed more concerned with her than anything in the woods. "You know how things have been shaking you lately. I've put you through too much, I'm sorry," he said, in a rare apology. "Let us deal with one matter at a time. It's quiet for now."

He kissed her on the forehead, surprising her, and his warmth against her even for a second was pleasing. But he continued forward.

This was, for her, one of those moments that quietly illuminated everything; she understood for the first time how it was that he got her into these situations. It was always "going to be fine"; it was endlessly "going to work itself out." He had a ready supply of calming words he used, and because things did always work out, he got away with talking her into dangerous places, and convinced himself that she liked them as much as he did. But what if it was not going to work out this time?

"Tobias, you feel different about this place. Why won't you just admit it?"

"I don't know what's happening," he said. "I can't protect you from this—you don't want me to say what I'm thinking."

The two strode into the forest without speaking. Tess tried to relinquish her worries; the people back there needed her.

She was deeply thankful that they hadn't gone far into the woods before coming upon a large house, old and defiant in the wilderness. A smaller, partly restored home clung beside it. There was nothing welcoming about either building; rather, the warped old windows seemed to absorb the pale light, leaving an impression of blackness in the structures. Snowflakes seemed to drift away from it at the last instant, and the rooftops gave off a strange aura of steam. The smell of wet spruce and fir had disappeared. An unseemly desolation enclosed Tess; she felt nearly devoid of sensation.

Reaching the smaller building she rapped on the door hurriedly. The little home was so quiet she could hear the distant shouts of the survivors behind her. Why couldn't the owner hear the terror that was happening outside?

Tobias went on to take a look at the larger house, and Tess was left alone.

Moving around the building, she saw no signs of life.

Driven by the desperate sounds behind her, she tried the door and found it unlocked.

She went in.

CHAPTER THIRTEEN

⌇⌇

The room was empty. Tess called out but no one replied. Predictably, the telephone reputed to be here was nowhere in sight. She was in what appeared to be an office. Bookcases lined the room, few of them full. The doctor must have only recently settled into the place. An examining table lay before her, with small icicles hanging from it.

Icicles. How long had the doctor's office been left like this, she wondered.

She glanced past the table to a cherrywood cabinet. She knew full well that it might contain medicines and any number of useful items, but there was something in its aspect that disturbed her. The cabinet's wood was carved with vines of roses that seemed to suggest faces, looking diabolical, half-completed, as if deformed or partly animalistic.

Not only sinister, the supply cabinet was a considerable disappointment compared to the telephone she'd hoped to find. The devices had blossomed across Massachusetts for nearly two decades, but they were still scarce in the countryside. Without one, Tess had to accept it was unlikely anyone would know for some time there was trouble.

She remembered the innkeeper, Mrs. Harnow, had wanted to come to the carnival. A woman like that would not let such a grand occasion pass her by. Mrs. Harnow's husband was a fireman; maybe she would bring him with her finally. And for that matter, couldn't the smoky bonfires they'd made be seen from Salem? They were far away, but it was possible.

The express was probably nearly an hour late or so already. Help would surely come, with or without a telephone.

Taking in a cool breath, she crossed the room.

The cabinet was empty.

Dispirited, Tess was about to leave the house when she saw a shadow in the corner of her eye.

It moved.

She turned. There was nothing to see.

It had been fast, whatever it was. She was staring in terror at the open door, the empty woods . . .

She could sense something in the room beside her. Someone had slipped in while she was busy with the cabinet. He was very close, giving off a kind of heat. But she would not confront him. *Be calm, you saw nothing,* she tried to convince herself.

She turned to leave—but whoever it was decided to come at her, rushing from the ink-dark shadows, pushing her against the wall.

It was the foreigner, Wilder. "Shh," he hissed.

"You."

"She is among us, *signora,*" he said, his eyes fixed on her, listening intently. "Here."

"There is nothing here," Tess protested.

"It is made to seem that way," said Wilder. His gigantic body was close against hers, and realizing it, he moved back. "You felt it also, did you not?" Tess wasn't sure what she felt, aware of nothing but the man alone. She wondered if he had somehow figured out her ability to sense the spirit realm.

Wilder ruminated for a moment, his eyes ransacking the house for danger. "I would not enter here. I thought it her homestead."

Tess frowned. "So you let me enter instead?"

"To test the waters."

"Test your *own* waters!"

Wilder's dark eyes betrayed no sympathy. "All goodness demands some sacrifice. . . ."

"Just what did that old man say to you? What is it exactly you're hunting here?"

"A thing of fairy tales and nursery rhymes." He held up a small book. "It's Salem's journal of the Magistrate," he explained. "Jurey gave it to me. It would seem he was part of a secret group, and on a mission of great importance."

He added, "The Salem witch trials had dealings with those who were far from innocent." His face was rigid with alertness. She could see his suspicion of the house persisted.

"There is only death in this place," she said.

"This is where the original Salem witches sought refuge," he said. "I falsely thought one remained: Old Widow Malgore. That's what Jurey called her. Not a woman at all, but a beast—it could be upon us at any moment."

His mood made Tess even more wary. "Your hands would be better suited to helping us."

Wilder looked offended. "My hands are in your service, *signora*. I do this for the good of all."

Just then Tobias came in. "The other house's doors are locked," he announced, looking displeased at Wilder, who seemed rather too close to his young wife.

"My search for a telephone was of no use," Tess replied.

Tobias didn't look at her. "Is Mr. Wilder . . . of some use?"

Wilder answered humorlessly. "I'm only interested in the body."

At this, Tobias raised an eyebrow. "I beg your pardon?"

Wilder turned and moved into the dark of the adjoining room. He pushed out a chair with a man's dead body in it, as if expecting to find it there. "The doctor," he explained.

Tess nearly gasped.

"She expects no resistance." Wilder smiled gravely.

She? Tess wondered. *The witch?*

"Jurey told me this would happen," he said. "The creature believes no one will challenge her. He told me that what we know of these things are mostly lies. . . ."

Wilder pulled a long, sickle-shaped dagger from the body. "To kill a wretch like this, you need a weapon of her own making to use against her." He held up the blade. "She's left us a means of destroying her. Careless, see that? Old Widow Malgore does not fear us."

Tobias watched him tensely. "Who did this murder?"

"I should think it obvious," said Wilder.

Tobias's composure barely cracked. "Mr. Wilder, you seem rather hasty in taking up Mr. Jurey's beliefs."

"Well, I met a man like Josiah Jurey once. An old Chinese in New York. He warned me that an assassin pursuing my employer was a woman skilled in witchcraft. I did not believe his words. And when she attacked—in an opium den, while we were vulnerable—I lost two very good friends in death. Thus, Mr. Goodraven, I never fail to listen closely when such men speak."

Suddenly, the dead figure fell forward. Its hand grasped Wilder's wrist tightly, shaking the dagger loose, and as Wilder fumbled with the convulsing man, his book fell to the floor.

Forcefully Wilder threw the dead man back and blasted the body twice with his pistol. Tess screamed. The body quivered and then wilted, ceasing all movement.

In the smoky quiet that followed, Tobias tried to seem calm and unimpressed, though Tess saw through the coolness of his bearing. "He may have been asking for help, you know," said Tobias.

Wilder shot a look at him. "He was dead."

"Ah. Thus the unnecessary *movement*?"

Wilder pocketed the dagger. "He was bewitched to take this from me. You saw it: the witch can reanimate death. . . ."

Tobias would not give in. "I've seen enough death to know we define it too simply. He may not have been dead at all."

"You, who says he has seen so much, have doubt of me?"

"I don't know what's happening here, Wilder, but I surely have doubts of you."

"A man without faith in man is a man who shall not see God," said Wilder.

"Another nugget of wisdom. And we owe you so much already," Tobias observed dryly, though he was rattled, and took a step to leave. "Amazing that someone like you could believe in anyone—you're hired to *dis*trust men, are you not?"

"You have no cause for distrust, I would think. I saved your life," said Wilder.

"Yes, from a dead man. Thank you so much, sir. Mr. Wilder, I'm no stranger to selfish pursuits, however odd, but whatever you're doing in this room, we could use your hulking mass for more pressing labors. You can help us get out of here, and fast."

The foreigner regarded Tobias sternly, as if surprised a young man could be so bold. Then he gazed at Tess calmly.

"We shall make the train a fortress," he said. "Then I will go after the beast."

CHAPTER FOURTEEN

r. Wilder moved so quickly it was as if he disappeared into the woods. By the time Tess and Tobias got back to the train, he was already there. Wilder, working with other men, had lifted a twisted piece of metal, setting free several people who were trapped in a car.

"Now we're getting somewhere," Tess observed. "The man is useful."

"If you like heroism," said Tobias, disdain in his voice.

Ahead, Sattler was carrying blankets. "Did you get help?" he hollered.

Tess shook her head slowly. "There's no telephone or telegraph. Nothing."

Tobias stepped closer to Tess. "Don't even try to explain. Not until we know for certain what's happening—"

"Mr. Goodraven, if you please," Sattler interrupted loudly. "Let's get these blankets to people, shall we?" He motioned emphatically to the growing congregation in the snow. As Tobias left to help, Tess turned to notice, between the joining of two train cars, several wounded passengers lying on the other side.

Hurriedly moving to that side of the train, she found bodies sprayed everywhere, thrown from a car. No help had yet reached the survivors over here.

She had expected to find that tawdry couple from the voyage's start, as she had not seen them since, well, since when? Since the accident, she thought. But what she found instead were travelers unknown to her.

Some of them shook strangely, their bodies almost burrowing into the snow. The sight was so unnerving Tess could not move for a moment. Perplexed, she finally knelt to aid the injured, looking back to see if anyone else was there to help her. But the train blocked her view and she realized she had lost track of Tobias.

Suddenly Annette was there—*had she been on this side all along?*—helping a young woman. Tess started to tell her the things she'd seen, but the words came out all wrong. It didn't matter; Annette was not the right person to speak to. Her innocent happiness had evaporated under the strain, her eyes were far away, her teeth clenched under cold, colorless lips.

Then Tess felt a sharp sting throughout her body, and knew instantly the emotion came from Tobias. He stood on her side of the train now, having brought two of the college boys with him, staring at something beyond the scattered debris.

Indeed, Tobias was stunned at what he saw. He couldn't believe his stupidity. Sattler followed his gaze. Then Michael.

"No . . . ," someone said. Across the white land, half blocked by a fallen tree, lay a lone train car, which had slipped from the snowbank, rolling away.

It was now on the lake, perched on the ice.

They could hear people crying out from inside.

Tobias and Sattler started running. They could see passengers through the frosted windows, banging for freedom—as the ice gave a sickening crack, splintering, spreading. Then the heavy car disappeared through the ice, consumed.

Tobias felt the breathless terror of dozens of people inside, their stomachs dropping as they plummeted into the cold depths. Nausea washed over him as he and the other young men ran for the hole in the ice where the train car had vanished.

Sattler cursed, helpless.

"If we go into that water, we're dead," said Michael.

"We could make it—" Ned argued.

"We don't know how deep it is. Or if we could even get people out."

Everyone was talking at once. Sattler felt the surface. "My God. It's so cold."

"We've got to have a try at it. We've got to try—"

"It's suicide, do you understand . . ."

In horror, they remained immobile. Tobias was sickened.

"I'm going in," Ned said.

Sattler looked at the stout young man. "No, you're not. You can't."

"They're going to die."

"They're already dead."

Tobias spoke up. "No. They're not."

Suddenly something burst from the water: A man, hands flailing, struggling to live. It was the stern father Tobias had seen at departure. Everyone rushed to help him, and Tobias caught his hand. But the weight was incredible; he couldn't pull him up—something had hold of him.

The man choked out, "Help me . . ." Another arm reached out of the water—an otherworldly, veined, bluish little arm. It clutched the man by the hair and pulled him down. Tobias was in shock. Everyone was yelling:

"What in God's name—"

"They were trying to get out—"

Tobias plunged his head and torso into the water. His eyes fell out of focus. He saw arms thrashing, blue and black, spinning ice. For an instant he was eye to eye with the father, and then suddenly was awash in ice fragments; he caught sight of the shocking figures of the man's furious daughters—dying—dead—blue-veined—faces grimacing.

Tobias could do nothing. The man's eyes were bulging, panicked. The girls were clinging to him with ferocious strength, fingers sinking into his clothes, as they all shot downward into the murky depths.

Still underwater, eyes blurring, Tobias had a moment to see what he thought was the sunken train car below, and all around it in the gray water, wispy figures flying, moving, swarming. There were two that parted from the rest and closed in on him—there was something different about them, but he could not make out what it was, just a feeling. One of them reached out to him, but as Tobias tried to see its face more clearly, a wave of lifeless thought came over him.

And then he was pulled up by Sattler and Michael.

CHAPTER FIFTEEN

I t all passed in a heartbeat.

Tobias, his skin nearly blue, gasped for air. Sattler and Michael began rubbing his face and upper body hard. Every vein in his body had turned to ice. He was painfully aware of blood pulsing throughout his entire system. His brain throbbed. He could feel his frozen eyes moving in their sockets. Through blurred vision, he saw Tess running toward him.

"Something down there . . . ," he moaned. Tess threw a heavy blanket around him.

"There are people down there . . . ," whispered Tobias.

The young men looked back at the large gash in the ice.

One of the older gentlemen began trudging toward them, warning them, "You can't go in there—there's nothing you can do for them." As he got closer, he looked at Tess. "You gotta get him warm. Get him out of those clothes, get him into one of these cars back there out of the wind."

The young men helped Tobias, half carrying him as he stumbled in the direction of the train. He looked back at the ice hole, but the passengers down there were surely dead now. He felt an absence of life, and Tess whispered to him, "No . . ." He knew that she meant they were gone, that she'd felt it, too. Tess had begun shaking, feeling the cold in his blood right along with him, her heart pounding.

Suddenly, Wilder was with them, and he hoisted Tobias over his shoulder, moving twice as fast as the other men, toward the train for shelter.

Wilder took him immediately to the caboose, and Tobias lay down on a bunk, wrapped under more blankets, surrounded by supply boxes. Annette joined Tess at his side.

The older man, who said his name was Carl, came with them, shooing off Wilder, Sattler, and the others. "He'll be all right; she'll tend to him. There are a lot of people we haven't even gotten to. Let's get working, gentlemen."

The door closed behind them. Tess frantically stripped off Tobias's shirts, rubbing his arms, trying to get the blood moving again, as Annette began searching the medical box for something useful. "I don't know what to do, I don't think anything will help him . . ."

"It's all right, it's going to be fine," said Tess, half in prayer.

Annette began mimicking Tess's actions, stroking Tobias's legs vigorously, until she realized in dazed horror what she was doing. Flushing red, she stared at Tobias's bare chest, her hands wrapped around one of his thighs. "I'm no nurse," she said blankly. Her fingers remained around his taut leg.

Mindlessly Tess pushed Annette's hands back. "I will see to him."

"I'm recovering," Tobias said weakly to Annette. "Honestly, go on. They need you out there. I'll be well and good in a moment."

Annette hesitated, but he seemed to be calming already, his shivering less violent. She left them alone in the car, though Tess scarcely noticed. "What happened to you out there?"

"I'm all right," he answered.

"Do you see? Do you see now? There is a devil in this place . . ."

"Shh, shh . . ." Now he was comforting her, leaning in to her, as she wrapped him in the blanket.

"You know it," said Tess. "You should've listened to me."

"There is something out there."

"I think I could feel it before we woke up, after the wreck. They were passing through us . . ."

"They?"

"The young man and the young woman from Salem," said Tess. "They were here, they were with us."

"There are so many dead here . . ."

"But the ones from Salem, Tobias. They would speak to us, they're different from the rest. . . ."

Tobias considered it, his body still rattled from the icy encounter. "I think there was one trying to reach me, someone different. Something kept him from . . . contact."

Tobias looked at Tess remorsefully, knowing he'd not been with her before, when she needed him and Tess forgave him instantly. She told him everything now, start to finish, wasting no time. "There is a rare power here," she said. "Did you not sense it? When that old man Jurey mentioned the Puritan couple—did you not feel what I did? It's so strange, Tobias. I've never felt anything like what's out there."

"Right now I don't feel anything out there."

Tess nodded. "Doesn't that scare you . . . ?"

Tobias looked at her a long moment. "Yes. It scares me very much."

Even without saying it, they knew that a force was at work in the woods, and it was toying with them, investigating, probing to see exactly what it was Tess and Tobias could sense.

Their feeling for what surrounded them had simply vanished, as if a great darkness had suddenly fallen over their secret senses, over their gift of sight. It occurred when he'd been pulled from the water, he thought.

"Tess, what do you think is happening? What is doing this to us?"

"A witch of Salem." Her voice quivered. It was the name Jurey had told them. "Malgore."

Tobias nodded, grim as a soldier. The fact of the witch's presence burned away any fairy-tale image in his head. "The spirits are warning us. The wretch is here."

"This is more than what you told me," Tess whispered. "You didn't tell me how terrible the risks were in all this."

"I didn't know. For all I'd heard about this little town, it might all have been rumor."

"It wasn't rumor."

He smiled at her weakly. "Well, I know that now."

"What do we do, Tobias?"

"Pray that someone's coming for us."

Far beyond the train wreckage, two carriages were working their way from Salem toward the winter carnival. The first belonged to the innkeeper Celia Harnow, and the second was that of a fire brigade, pulled by fresh horses. The men aboard, including her husband, had been ill-disposed toward coming, but Mrs. Harnow had convinced her husband to investigate why phone and telegraph service to Blackthorne had been mysteriously severed in the past few hours.

Naturally, Celia's true motive was to end up at the festivities, and Rupert, her driver, was grumbling at the rough shortcut they had chosen. It was very cold out here.

As the coach rounded a curve on the long-neglected road, one of the horses slipped on some ice, and Rupert struggled for control. When he looked up, the road was covered in a thick mist.

"Whoa!"

He could no longer see the fire brigade ahead in the bank of mist, but he could hear it. Men shouting, horses screaming, then a crackling sound like lightning, a pounding, wreckage, and splintering wood.

Celia hit the floor of the carriage as Rupert strained to slow the horses. She could see only a screen of ivory fog outside. They crawled onward, and Celia could make out pieces of the gnarled trees nearby, their grotesque shapes flashing from the ocean of white. She had long lived near this patch of wilderness, but never had the woods felt so threatening until this moment. Terrified for her husband, she eased her head out the window.

Horses squealed somewhere in the fog. A huge tree had toppled over, crushing the fire wagon, and the men—her husband among them—lay strewn about, staring upward, bloodied, their faces and bodies crushed.

Celia's heart nearly stopped. "Good Jesus," she whispered.

"Jesus," echoed Rupert, and he pulled on the reins, but a twisted tree branch near him seemed to uncurl and whip around his neck like a living thing—yanking him, writhing, into the air. Celia saw him thrown back, heard the cracking of his neck. The horses bolted, and Celia's carriage jumped forward, rumbling past the accident. She looked out, frantic, but couldn't jump. The road was rushing under the coach too fast.

Suddenly, something leaped before the coach. A skeletal, white-haired beast in tatters was clinging above the carriage, staring at her upside down through the window, a hoarse voice wheezing incomprehensibly.

Celia was stunned.

The thing darted out of view. Then suddenly—as the coach emerged from the mist—the road curved. The carriage ripped free of the horses and was flung sidelong over a snowy embankment, into a ravine.

In pain, Celia lifted her head. It took her a moment to realize the window was full of snow. She turned. All the windows were snow-blocked.

Mother of God.

She was trapped alive.

"Oh no . . . no, no, no . . ."

She couldn't open the door. The coach's front lay under the snow. Snow on all sides of her, from the carriage's collapse into the ravine. She pulled at the other door. Frantic, she kicked it over and over but it would not budge.

A voice whispered in her ear, close, the breath tickling her hair, "She's not going to hear us . . . She's not going to hear us . . ."

Celia kicked more violently—screeching for help.

But the voice did not speak again.

She tried to be calm. Even her breath seemed loud. She smashed at the window glass, and a wall of snow greeted her. Suddenly, to her shock, the snow moved and a face pushed out of it, a young woman, dressed in long-ago Puritan fashion.

Celia screamed and dived down, but when she looked up the face was gone, and there was nothing but silence around her.

She patted her chest, trying to recover. She began clawing at the snow, trying to get free, but then she turned, and was startled to see the young Puritan woman inside with her. The youthful figure glistened in the light, turning into a mistlike spirit that began weaving its fingers into Celia's chest, a vapor reaching into her.

Shrieking, Celia clambered to the other side of the carriage, but the space was too small, too confining. There was nowhere to go.

The young woman was hissing, "She will take your spine . . . She will take it . . ."

Celia screamed.

The woman persisted. "There is but one way to kill her . . . No—God—she follows—"

Abruptly, the Puritan woman shredded into nothingness, her misty flesh grinding away in an instant, falling into Celia in terror.

And then her awareness of everything slipped away.

★ ★ ★

She did not see the other presence, the skeletal white-haired Thing, the Malgore wretch, lurking in the forest, her clawed hand angrily tearing at a tree. The bark crackled in her fingers as if it had been touched by white lightning, and it bled from her in ashes. The witch had lost her hold on the carriage, and she was seething with a hellish, inhuman fury.

CHAPTER SIXTEEN

❧

For Tess and Tobias, closed off inside the caboose, the other survivors were now only a din of troubled voices out in the snow. Tobias had improved. His breathing was normal, his skin was warming. Amid the supply boxes, he and Tess huddled close, puzzling over what had happened in cautious whispers.

"I think I know what it intended," Tobias was saying, "the spirit in the water. There *was* something special about that one; it tried to touch my eyes. It was trying to tell me something, and then I felt its words taken, blocked, as if walled off from my senses. I could almost say a spell came over me."

He shuddered. "Malgore is keeping them from us. The two cannot reach past her . . . That's what the spirit meant for me to know. Malgore is the one: the mother who forbade the marriage of that couple in Salem. Malgore was the First Accused, the unnamed in the books. What's happening here is . . . we've stumbled into a blood feud."

His mind turned it over. "It's just as Jurey said—the three remain here, the lovers and that madwoman, locked in hateful conflict."

Tess remained quiet. Something *was* trying to get to her, she thought, the spirits of the young man and woman from Salem, but she didn't want to receive their words. She should've heeded her own intuition to stay away. *Learn to listen to life's subtle warnings.*

"Something pulled me from the train," she repeated.

Tobias murmured assent. "When I woke, my head was inches from a shaft of metal that should easily have pierced my brain. We are being protected. We have been from the moment we got here."

"Then they want something from us. What is it?"

"What do spirits always want?" said Tobias. "They want to be listened to. They want justice."

"How do we give it to them?"

He looked at her, thinking. They had answered a call, and now they had been discovered. A task was being prepared for them, and both knew that they were going to be instruments in this battle, vital to some cause.

Tess remembered: "Jurey tried to warn me. He said they want something. He said to find what it is that gives them power, and seize it from them. He must have meant all three who were hanged here in Blackthorne, but it's Malgore we have to be concerned with. She is the darkness here, clearly the most powerful of them. We *just* have to figure out what these spirits are saying."

Tobias met her eyes. He knew he had made a profound mistake in coming to this place. "Tess. We have to get *out* of here."

Outside, many of the survivors were gathered on the snow. They seemed to fear returning to the damaged cars. Some were shaking from the cold, others were passing blankets in a long line to those too injured to be moved from their train cars.

Sattler brought new clothes for Tobias, peeled from a dead man. Tobias took them with macabre amusement. Dressed in a dry suit, he emerged from the car caboose, lifting Tess gallantly to the ground, while other women noted this gentlemanly act as if it were a reminder civilization could exist even here. The couple joined the large group of survivors who were standing, numb and silent, beside the tracks. With the urgent wounds of the injured dressed as well as possible, it was clear the early work was over. No one knew what to do now.

Wilder remained at the edge of the battered camp, vigilant, his eyes on the woods.

No one had yet found the couple Tess referred to as the Tawdrys. Perhaps they had gone back into one of the train cars or had wandered into the woods and collapsed from their injuries. Tess felt guilty for judging them earlier.

A small group stood together at the rear of the train comprised of the college boys and some other travelers. The Goodravens completed the circle. Gil, whose birthmark looked like war paint in the bright white surroundings, glanced at Tobias and broke the silence. "You're lucky. There are a lot of dead here, unh? Johnson. Hargreave. Mr. Halfstead's gone. Cut in two."

Tobias looked gravely at the milky sky. "Imagine the chances," he said. "His name was *Half*stead, for God's sake."

Gil glanced over. "What's that? Sir, have you something to say?"

Tobias drew a long breath. "We can't stay here long," he said. "We need to be moving. There's little chance for some of these people."

"Hey now, fellow, we're going to be just fine," Gil answered sharply. "We're going to pull together. By the end of it, people are going to tell stories about how courageous we all were, and how we never lost faith in . . . faith in our God or ourselves."

Tobias looked to the group. "Anyone else feel that optimistic?"

Who could fail to love him, thought Tess.

"No one is coming," a woman muttered. "It's nearly noon now, more than two hours since the accident. When the train didn't arrive, there should have been alarms sounded, wires sent out. What is going on in town? There is telephone service already in Salem and Blackthorne—why isn't there any help coming . . . ?"

Ned looked at Sattler. "Exposure like this, I mean to say . . . the cold . . . it can affect what you see, right?" Sattler nodded, uncertain.

"A rescue party's been sent out by now, I'm sure of it," a man was saying.

Everyone was speaking at once.

"The storm is getting worse, it could be holding them up."

"It's not that bad."

"Why else would they be staying back?"

A woman, wild-eyed, unsteady, moved toward the group. "I think we need to go right now, go and get help."

Tobias looked down the tracks. "How far are we from the carnival?"

"Oh, I don't know. I'd say six miles," Carl answered.

"Maybe less. Four miles or so," said another man, "given how long we were aboard the train."

"How far back to civilization?"

The mountain man, Carl, his ill-fitting suit torn and bloodstained, conferred with another man. "What do you think?"

"A good deal more, surely."

"All right, then, if we're closer to Blackthorne, we go on to the carnival," Tobias concluded.

"We should've sent someone already," a man named Alan grumbled to himself.

Tobias said, "Well, we need help fast. And no one seems to be coming."

"They'll be here," Gil's wife, Elaine, spoke up. "The roads might be worse off than we think. . . ."

"It could be some time. They might not know how dangerous this is. They might just think the train stopped working," Carl said.

"We'll never know," said Tobias, "unless we get going." He looked at them all expectantly.

There it is, thought Tess, *he's said it*.

"I can protect you," said an accented voice. It was Wilder, who had joined them without being noticed. Everyone looked up at the giant man.

Tobias was pleased. "All right. Who else?"

Sattler nodded to Tobias. "I'm with you, I don't like sitting about here and waiting."

Tess realized it was inevitable. He was going to leave. They would be separated. "In such weather, it could take hours . . . ," she said.

"I'm in good condition, I think I can handle it," Tobias said to the group.

"Not many others look like they're up to it," remarked Sattler.

Gil said, "It's a job for the young."

Ned looked at everyone staring him down. "I'm too fat to walk far. If I stay here and die, they can feed off my body for days."

He seemed to be serious, and Tobias gave him a deadpan glance. "Now that's an attractive offer. Maybe I'll stay."

But Sattler was ready to move. "We'll take Michael with us."

Michael suddenly turned ashen, evidently in no mood to be a hero. "What? Why don't we let people volunteer for this job?" His eyes went to Annette for help, but she offered none.

Tess pulled Tobias away. "You can't do it. I don't want you to go out there."

Tobias put his hands on her shoulders. "No one has yet come for us, and we've waited long enough. I don't want us to be trapped at nightfall. You can go with me . . ." He motioned over his shoulder, to the woods along the tracks. "Or stay here."

Neither option seemed remotely appealing to Tess. Those trees in the snow were like a vast row of teeth, and they were going to swallow her, they were going to tear her apart. She had no doubt of it.

"I don't like the way this feels," she said. "Going out there scares the devil out of me."

"You know I have to go, Tess."

"You don't have to do anything."

"Have a look at this group. Most of them are too old or too hurt to walk that far in good conditions, let alone in a storm. Someone has to go, and I think we both know I've a better chance at handling this . . . special situation. Look at Sattler. Look at the pale one, Michael. You think they could deal with what's out there?"

"What makes you think *you* can cope with it?"

"Tess, this feeling that we have, it could be posturing. This witch, this entity, could simply be angry at us for entering its domain and . . . this could all be nothing."

"You know it isn't nothing."

He smiled. "It could be we're completely insane. I'm not confident of my grasp on reality on any day, but after all that shaking and crashing, my brain is probably a soufflé."

She held her voice tightly in control. "Can you trust me that this is not the way? Something will happen to you, I feel it. Don't be pigheaded—"

"I feel exactly the same way if we stay here. I have to do something. I have to."

"You enjoy this."

"You can't blame me for these circumstances."

"I can." She tried to smile. "It's how I know you'll come back and make up for it."

"You could come with me," Tobias suggested. "You could make this journey, I'm sure of it."

"I'm not."

"You can do it, Tess, you know you can."

"Out in the open?"

"Our life is one long train wreck, isn't it? Fires and tragedies . . . you can face anything." He laughed nervously. "The woods here aren't going to beat you. There's just less light in there, that's all. We'll walk right past them, and stay along the tracks."

"It's not darkness that frightens me, it's the openness, getting lost. . . . We would be away from everything," she said. "They need me here. I can help people if I stay."

"Then stay."

"Keep yourself together. Don't lose hope, Tobias."

"I'm not made that way; you can't lose what you never had." Tobias kissed her cheek. "Decision's made. Now, let's just get through it, quick as we can."

Alarmed, she pulled him back to her. "Is that all I get? A peck on the cheek?"

He leaned in close, whispering in her ear, "If I could romance you here and now, I would, dearest, but it wouldn't fit with the public image. Be strong."

"I want a promise you'll be back."

"One way or another, I will." He smiled and stepped away.

Incredibly, he was going to leave her.

CHAPTER SEVENTEEN

He was leaving, that was the end of it. Tess immediately had second thoughts, but they'd made the only responsible move. She suddenly hated everyone around her for making her be responsible.

"Let's move out," said Tobias, and though he was the youngest, the two college men and Wilder did as he said. "We'll be back as soon as we can."

Tess gripped her dress tightly. Again she wanted to stop him, but he was moving quickly off into the snow, his familiar tall-fellow slump so endearing. Why wouldn't he look back? This was a mistake; the two of them were not meant to be apart. Even the air smelled of a violation of the order of things. Something unnatural was unfolding.

Setting out northward, toward the Blackthorne carnival, Michael, Sattler, and Tobias marched through the snowfall, beside the tracks. Wilder followed them, providing a watchful guard.

They crossed the blood-drenched snow near the engine, passing the wild elk corpses. These disgusted the other men, but Tobias found them enthralling. To him, death was intriguing in all its forms. He didn't care for it as a personal experience, though he could probably be convinced to give it a try. He found little enough reason to get up in the morning, and if it weren't for Tess, there would be no reason at all. He would not look back at her.

He'd avoided telling her about the feeling that his father and mother were woven into this mystery in some manner. Tess could probably tell he was lying, but he knew her well enough to guess the conclusion she'd come to; that he was hiding a lack of faith in their chances. Ever the pessimist.

He was perfectly aware there was something in the woods, pulling him in, but he doubted there was any way to avoid it. If death was coming, it would be yet another adventure to fascinate him before fascination faded for good.

Blending with the whiteness of the forest, a figure watched the scene of devastation. The form was motionless and the only life within came from its eyes. Its ivory flesh, embroidered with slow-pulsing veins, was of a piece with the bark of the trees and the reflective snow.

It had made itself unseen. An observer staring into the woodlands would be hard-pressed to find anything there.

The creature's deformed appearance was the work of centuries, the sculpting hand of time, and the aftereffects of lurid magic. A starved and hollow-eyed creature once known as Widow Malgore, she had little human quality left to her. She, and every other presence in the forest, were acutely conscious that Tess was now separated from Tobias, and the couple weakened by isolation.

The Thing, the witch of Salem, darted away, deeper into the woods. It moved around to see Tobias Goodraven and the other young men heading away. It could see Wilder's guns and Indian occult trinkets swinging at his belt. The skin near the creature's eyes wrinkled in angry displeasure.

It lingered, silent as snowfall.

Annette and Tess watched their partners go. Tobias moved with more surety than the others, with a certain grace on the glistening and difficult ground.

But it was just as Tess had feared: there was no help coming, and now Tobias was leaving. She told herself that if they got out of this, they would never seek out such darkness again. It had once been worth the risk; now she feared that she had, like her husband, grown to need these moments of heightened existence. She'd gotten what she deserved, she thought.

Annette broke the silence. "He's quite an unusual person."

"Women often remark upon it."

"How long have you been together?"

"Forever. And since we've been married, we've spent no more than a few nights apart. He's my anchor, you know, I think I need him."

"It won't be long."

"I'm afraid that it will."

Annette looked at her, sympathetic. "The others are with him. He'll be back before nightfall." Tess wanted to strangle her, and yet loved her at the same time for trying. "My fiancée, Sattler, will look after him."

Fiancé. Annette said nothing of Michael's special attention to her. Tess wondered if the girl was even aware of their rivalry.

Shivering, Ned walked over to them. He shook his chubby

face like a wet Saint Bernard. "If it gets any colder, I may need to hide under your petticoats. It's strictly survival, I assure you."

Tess ignored his joke, looking over the wreckage surrounding them. She needed to occupy her mind. "I think we need to set up a central place, move everyone together where it's warm," she said to the group. "It appears there's no danger of fire now. If you look toward the rear of the train, it seems to me the parlor cars are the least damaged; I know there's not enough room for all of us, but if we share the time inside . . ."

"Yes," said one of the men, seeing where she was headed. "We'll put the wounded who can move in there. The rest of us can rotate in for the privilege. That'll do for now."

"That's where we'd be the most comfortable," Gil agreed.

Tess added, "Correct me if I'm wrong, but there are woodstoves in those back cars, right?"

"Yes."

"We need to keep them running, don't you think? It'd be a good thing to keep people's minds busy as well." She looked at the men, hoping for agreement.

"All right, let's be at it," said Alan. He shouted to the others, organizing the wood gathering and the stoking of bonfires to warm those who couldn't fit in the crowded parlor cars.

Tess estimated a hundred or so survivors remained out on the snow, plus two dozen with significant injuries, and perhaps twenty still inside the train cars, unable to be moved. With the flow of travelers around her, it was hard to get a fix on the exact numbers, which only raised her anxiety.

Under Alan's supervision, the men had begun to work together.

Most were elderly, though Tess recognized they were in a more rugged state of fitness than she first observed.

She made a quick study of them. There were two friends, Carl and Leo, in their forties; Carl, mountain-hardened, with a beer belly and cowboy mustache, was a tall, rough-hewn man, his low voice a comfort to many of the wounded. He's had something to drink already this morning, she realized. His companion Leo was smaller, balding, with thick glasses, and seemed more thoughtful. He appeared to be Indian, or partly of that ancestry.

She detected a strong smell of horses on them, as well as a lack of comfort with other human beings. Carl had about him the pale radiance of regret, a kind of dim light around him that never departed. As they headed to the forest edge to collect fallen branches and cut firewood, Carl stumbled, and Leo righted him. He looked at Tess. "He hasn't been himself since we sent the horses up," Leo said. "The animals *knew.* Something was wrong. We sent them up to Blackthorne with his brother all the same. We shouldn't have done that."

Tess was right: the two had more comfort with horses than with people. These men had been warned somehow, in a small way. What was it that animals sensed, which people could not? No one ever heeded that vague cautioning . . .

She turned her attention to the others.

Alan was a bearlike fellow, more of a growl to him, impatient; Tess saw Navy tattoos on his forearm when he examined his own injuries. Gil was a bit softer, his gray hair swept back diligently above that painful-looking port-wine mark. He looked more frail than most here, but he had a sharp mind. His wife, Elaine, was strong and optimistic; you could see she looked after Gil constantly.

None of them wore their fear on their sleeves.

Tess looked at Annette and Ned. "We have to take a look and see who it's safe to move. If we can't move them, we'll have to take turns in getting them hot drinks, keeping them warm."

She glanced at the woods. "And no one goes anywhere alone."

CHAPTER EIGHTEEN

As the day drifted uneasily into early afternoon, Tobias and the others tramped on, the snow clutching their ankles with every heavy step.

"I wouldn't want to be back there, holed up in a train car," Sattler was saying. "Annette won't take it well. How do you think yours will fare in this situation?"

"Well, there's no fear of enclosed spaces for Tess," Tobias answered. "She'd never leave home, if she could get away with it. I practically have to pull her out. She has a level mind under duress, for the most part. I think she'll be all right."

"Have you ever been through something like this before, Mr. Goodraven?"

"Feels like a thousand times," said Tobias. "Actually, the truth is, we go looking for this sort of thing. But this is the worst I've ever been through."

Sattler stared at him. "You were serious, then. I mean, about being . . . ghost . . . hunters?"

Tobias nodded. "It's better than most vices. Though it does affect one in most peculiar ways."

"And what does that mean?" Sattler looked confused. "Have

you some kind of disease, you two?"

Tobias looked askance at him. "It's not catching."

"Well, what is it, then?"

"We just have a condition that affects certain people, when spirits have passed through them a number of times."

Sattler looked at him as if he were completely insane. Tobias continued, unfazed, "You feel emotions washing over you, thoughts, ideas. If this happens many times, well, you sort of get to know where they are. You see?"

"No, I don't see at all."

"Tess and I, we have a special condition. It develops over time. We feel the presence of those no longer with us."

Sattler seemed unsure what to make of this statement. Tobias kept walking, quite comfortable.

Up ahead, he spied a heap of black cloth upon the snow.

"What the devil . . . ," muttered Sattler.

On the ground was the slick-looking gentleman who had earlier targeted Tess with his inappropriate gaze. He lay beside his wife, the woman whose clothing was cheap and ostentatiously ornamented. The two were clearly dead, though how they'd gotten that way was open to question.

"Tawdry situation, this," said Michael, adjusting his spectacles.

"What were they doing out here?" Sattler wondered aloud.

"Selfish pair, they went off for town together. They left the train," conjectured Michael. "Didn't want to help anyone and delay their own chance of survival."

Tobias said nothing, examining the snow-covered bodies.

"So what did they die of?" returned Sattler. "They look perfectly unharmed."

"It could've been head injuries that did them in, right?" Michael asked, backing up a bit, staying clear of the dead.

"Could have been," said Sattler. "Maybe they wandered off not knowing how bad their injuries were. . . ."

The couple's hands were locked together. A final gesture, perhaps.

"Very strange," said Tobias finally.

Wilder's brown eyes glided to him pointedly. "It is."

"Nothing to be done about it now." Tobias decided. "Let's move on."

"And not even cover them?" Sattler rebuked him.

"You may leave your coat if you like," said Tobias, continuing onward.

There was nothing to be done, but Sattler seemed annoyed by the comment, and furthermore at Tobias's seizing of leadership again, his driving their pace. "You *wanted* to see death," he said finally. "Isn't that what you said? You came for this. All of us here are just part of the theater of the thing, aren't we?"

Tobias answered, "Yes, well, I'm not very close to other people, if that's what you mean. It wasn't bravery that got me out here. All of that sickening human need everywhere at the train—I was starting to lose my mind."

"Starting to?" Michael muttered.

Tobias could feel their doubts about him, like a mild buzzing in his brain, but he was unperturbed. He was accustomed to New

York, teeming with grudges and bitterness.

"Ghosthunting . . . it's a very interesting way to spend your time," said Sattler skeptically.

Tobias waited for more. What did they think his true reasons for being here were?

"I suppose tragedies in general are a lot of fun for you," Sattler added.

"Most of the time they are," Tobias replied in anger. "But then there's wonderful occasions like this, with all that screaming and dying. It would make anyone happy, wouldn't it?"

He left out that he could feel the pains—and secrets—of Sattler and Michael as well.

Sattler seemed to grow more curious. "Well, what made you decide to . . . I mean, why did you ever start to seek out such things?"

Tobias paced on, the snow sludging underfoot. "The first time, I was seeking my mother and father—and so was Tess. Both of our parents had died in a theater fire. That's how we met. We were looking for a medium who could connect us with our families." He drifted off, remembering.

"Well?"

"Well, it was partly successful. We had a séance, and the entire room caught fire. I connected with my father's ghost, but just for a moment. At least I think it was him. He called me a wretched little good-for-nothing, so that's a clue."

Tobias could tell Michael did not want this conversation to go further. He clearly figured Tobias for a madman.

Sattler pressed. "Father was a bit of a tyrant?"

"Not really. But he thought of me as slothful."

"Interesting," Wilder remarked. "My father took such a view of me as well. I'd nearly forgotten those words." He looked pensive. "It almost seems as if he's with me now. Calling me forward out here, even in death."

The others all glanced back at him. "You have that feeling?" asked Tobias.

Wilder was reticent. "I feel something. Since we got here."

In that instant, Tobias mused that perhaps all along what he had felt in the forest, this calling from the other side, was nothing more than death itself, a lingering bounty of decay rising like mist, and Tobias had merely associated the sensation of death and loss with his own family.

He figured Wilder could have simply done the same. When one thinks of death, one thinks of lost loved ones, the explanation was nothing more than that. Tobias burned. He felt a bigger fool than ever. There was nothing special here for him.

"So is that what keeps you looking?" Sattler continued, not sure if Tobias was pulling his leg. "The search for your parents in the afterworld?"

"No. It's just that Tess and I seemed to have a knack for it. We started to seek out hauntings, and then it just got so wickedly interesting. You get to feeling things you never felt, and then you get to wanting the sensation again and again. Ordinary life becomes a bore."

Wilder said nothing.

"What I can't figure out is how you two came together," Michael said abruptly to Tobias. "She seems such an elegant girl . . ."

"Tess? Oh, we're torn from the same cloth. She's . . . well, she's everything. She's my heart and my lungs. And my liver and my bowels," he quipped.

Michael groaned. "Lovely."

Wilder glanced at Tobias, tainting the air with envy.

"We've become so close now, I can feel her even at this distance. I can feel her . . . fear," said Tobias, his confidence slightly fading. He *could* feel her still, but their link was weakening. "Tess and I have been through quite a lot together. When we read about this—witches of Salem, fugitives, tortured and hanged—who could resist such an encounter?"

"I could have," muttered Sattler.

"No, I don't think you could. You're the most hypocritical one in the bunch," Tobias said flatly. The wind hissed around them as they trekked onward.

Wilder watched them with special care, a man used to conflicts spilling out of control.

"I'm afraid I don't know what you mean, sir," Sattler replied, caught off-guard.

"You're lying," Tobias said. "It has to do with what's in the pack. What *is* in the pack? You couldn't leave it on the train . . . ? I even left my cello, for heaven's sake."

Sattler looked at Tobias, caught. "You're going to think I'm . . . something of a disgusting fellow."

Tobias feigned shock. "You think so?"

Sattler frowned and handed Tobias his satchel, allowing him to take a look inside. Tobias rifled through the contents: sketches and rolled-up paintings.

"What of it? It's art. Michael's an art student, is he not?" Tobias could sense Sattler was a good person despite his lapses, and the young man folded under his gaze.

"These are . . ." It seemed hard for Sattler to say it. "These are sketches by murderers. Reputedly by Jack the Ripper, the New York Garroter, people like that. I sell them. They're worth a lot of money."

Tobias looked them over with interest, and then he found what looked like a child's mitten.

"Some of these things come from murder victims," explained Sattler. "It's perverse, but there are people who pay for this kind of object. I actually thought you might be doing the same business here, and I was pressing you to find out. This place could be a treasure trove."

Sattler averted his eyes. "So, we were coming to get some wood splinters from the old town before it's too late, and maybe some remains from the witch-killings. Those articles would be worth something."

Wilder looked disgusted, and Michael and Sattler clearly felt embarrassed. Michael kept his gaze fixed on a far-off point. But Tobias was fascinated. "Well . . . you're much sicker than I am! You two are going straight to hell." He said it like it was a compliment.

He handed back the satchel and walked onward, as Sattler called after him. "It's not as if we like this. I have to pay off one of my teachers or he'll flunk me out of Harvard. I knew a fellow, and I just got started in this . . ."

Tobias kept walking, uninterested.

"My sketches don't pay real well, you see?" said Michael, regretful.

For con men, they were awfully sorry for themselves. Have some *conviction,* thought Tobias.

"The money's a great temptation. We're going to get twenty dollars just for their effects," Sattler added.

Tobias stopped. "Whose?"

"Well, that Salem couple, the ones who fled to Blackthorne," said Sattler. "This is all that was left of them. I got it from one of the Boston investors. He wanted to be rid of the stuff."

He was holding up a small box. Tobias took it from him. Inside were tatters of lace, two candles, and two wedding rings.

"What naughty children," Tobias commented. "Rings were not allowed by the Puritans." Married couples used to exchange thimbles; girls would get creative, defy their fathers, and work the metal into rings. Tobias was touched by the sight of someone's precious keepsakes, and he decided to dislike Sattler even more for having the box. "These things belonged to Malgore's daughter and the German, the two from Salem?"

"Yes."

"This is not the sort of thing someone like you should have."

"I came to get more. You're not going to take it from me. . . ."

Tobias pushed the box away, bothered by it. "Oh, no. No, it's yours. But I think it *is* valuable. No telling who would want it. You hold on to it tight."

Tobias walked off, leaving the other three to follow. *Find out what gives them power, and seize it,* old man Jurey had said.

Beware the art student with no money, Tobias told himself. "Well, I'm glad Tess didn't hear this. All she wanted was to be somewhere at Christmas . . . where it was *peaceful.*"

CHAPTER NINETEEN

❧

Snow floated down gently, but tranquility was nowhere else in evidence this afternoon. Of the 240 original passengers, 183 were still alive. The survivors were mostly collected in those cars at the portion of the train still on the tracks; the wounded lay in overstuffed chairs, the grand parlor made eerie by their presence. Some lay on the floor. Others sat beside them, offering comfort. Tess checked to be sure everyone in her car was being cared for, and then passed through the doorway into the next car.

There she saw more wounded, more agony. Ned was tending to the injured, but he stepped over to Tess, and spoke quietly, with a trembling, embarrassed smile across his doughy face. "Strangest thing. I keep feeling a breath on my back, like someone's there . . ."

It was the last thing she wanted to hear. "We're all a little rattled. We need more water. I'm going to the dining car," she said.

She couldn't get out fast enough, her empathic sense overwhelming her. She felt the physical pain of everyone around her: she crossed past a leg injury, her legs stung; she walked past a gouged eye, her vision blurred.

These people had meant nothing to her before; now her well-being was tied up in them almost literally.

"I think we should find the ones related to the Salem witch-hunters, and throw them outside," said Ned, a touch of unwelcome gallows humor. And then he tiredly yelled after her, "Get us more whiskey for the wounded if you can, Tess."

"It's the only tonic for pain that we have left," said Gil, catching her sleeve, "and there's no telling how long we'll be out here, unh?"

"I'll do my best."

Tess crossed into the dining car, a soft oasis.

Annette was sitting at a table, and near her some of the women were huddled around coffeepots and teakettles, perhaps a dozen others simply resting, taking in the warmth from the woodstoves. Everyone looked at Tess guiltily, and she felt sorry to always be driving them on, like some impossible wartime nurse.

"Come over, get yourself a couple seconds' rest," said Elaine, opting to bring her into their small rebellion. It struck Tess again that Gil's wife gave off such youthful energy. Attuned to her now, Tess understood that rather than being odd, she simply had no real awareness that she was no longer young.

Another, much older woman, Lucinda, a grand Southern dame, who was managing to look impressive and composed even now, introduced herself and poured some coffee. "Get yourself warmed up," she said kindly.

Tess accepted, and felt a strange sensation coming off them, not quite warmth—there was too much distress for that—but stillness, at least.

Lucinda smiled. "I was telling Elaine this place ought to be more famous than it is, all the business that's gone on around it." She had a great storytelling voice, and Tess sat unmoving, clutching the steaming coffee, listening with interest. "It's just not a place that gives up its dead. Which I take as a good sign. If I die, I want it to be right here . . . where I can live on in some form." She laughed, becoming thoughtful. "You know, they tried running this train before . . ."

The wind became audible outside, a low distressed hum. "What happened?" Tess asked nervously. She felt the interest of the other women around the car rising.

"Well, the first time they tried to run it, not twenty years ago, when the tracks were new, it got trapped under the snow just past Blackthorne. Except for a little smokestack, the whole train was lost under a blanket of snowfall. Covered up like a babe in a cradle. They wired for help. Told everyone, you just sit tight. I imagine it wasn't too terrible at first. They had first-class accommodations. . . . People bringing you hot cocoa and little English cookies, roasted duck and what have you . . . waiting however many days 'til someone came to dig you out."

"This actually happened here? The entire train buried?" Tess marveled. "What became of the people?"

"For two days a blizzard raged here," said Lucinda. "The men that dug it out found everyone dead. Blood on the furniture. The children had been locked in cars away from their folks. Curious thing, as if those people wanted to protect children from themselves. Lord knows what took place. The young ones died of fright, they thought.

"Whatever the reason, *something* happened down there. Spooked the rescuers so bad they made quick work of cleaning up, and never ran the train after that. Figured someone didn't want them coming this way. That simple."

Elaine was a tough-minded, practical New Englander, but the Southern woman's story caused her to shudder. "It was a lot of terrible luck. It can't be more than that."

"Used to be folks had no reason to come up here," added Lucinda. "Now we got a reason. Our big celebration, our 'grand defiance' of winter and of being closed off from each other and of . . . death . . ."

Painfully, Annette reflected on some private memory, and seeing Tess regard her, she admitted, "I keep thinking there are so many little questions I've had for Sattler, so many talks I wish I'd had with him before now."

Tess smiled. "Where he'd like to live, how many kids someday . . ."

"Yes. Well . . . well, not that. I mean to say, I can't have children, so that doesn't come up much."

Tess nodded, and Annette added rather nervously, "I'd just as soon you didn't tell anyone. Sattler has a great interest in starting a family, and I'd rather be the one to tell him. He's a very understanding person, though. You can count on Sattler for most anything. If he were here, I feel we'd all be in much better shape."

There was an awkward pause, and Lucinda broke in, "Y'all need to worry less, rely less on your men. I never had need of one in sixty-eight years. We're going to be fine out here now, you just watch."

"How ever did someone like you end up here?" Tess asked her. She admired the woman; to be striking out on her own at such an age must have taken courage.

Lucinda smiled. "Well, I wanted to live out my final years in a new place, somewhere quiet. I am sick of Southern men and Southern drink, and I am sick of the heat in Atlanta."

"We have heat in New England," countered Elaine.

"Not like Atlanta. It's Southern heat. It comes with drunkenness and public carrying-on," Lucinda said. "And I wasn't about to put up with the noise and the arrogance of Boston or New Haven or Providence. Blackthorne has itself some history. I confess a fascination with it, and it's cheap to get somewhere to live."

"I wish you'd been in my train car earlier," Elaine said. "We might have had a lot to talk about."

"You have a husband?"

"Yes."

"Well, he'd have shut you up, and we wouldn't have talked. That's the way it is."

Elaine laughed. "Gil isn't so bad. He's a thinker. He likes facts. He's spooked by all this, and he hates to say it. He might grumble a bit, but he cares for me. The man I'd wanted to marry when I was younger was a brute to his wife, I found out later. I was lucky Gil found me, and I didn't know it 'til now, as I sit here thinking about it. You can forgive a lot in a man, if you know the other hand you might've been dealt."

"I don't want to have to forgive a lot," murmured Tess.

"If you want perfect, my dear, you're not going to find it in this life," Elaine replied. For an instant, a veneer of violet tickled Tess's vision, a hue that signified hope. Elaine, it seemed, had hope for her husband to change, even at her age.

We come in and out of fooling ourselves, Tess thought. That must be how it's done over the long haul.

Wind shook the windows. Tess looked around the car, spooked by a new chill entering the space.

"I feel like something is opening up . . . ," she said, sickened. The women stared at her, blankly. She looked around for a source. "Something's with us. It's on the train. Right now."

The women kept staring, their expressions unclear.

Tess took in a breath of the cold air, wishing for Tobias. But he was not here, and try as she might, she could not feel him near her anymore. For all she knew, he was dying. Or already dead.

CHAPTER TWENTY

S omething was hunting Tobias. The tremors he'd felt in
the past had never been quite this persistent. Many spirits
seemed at first unremarkable, he had learned; they had only
the same tenacious need to hold on to an old reality. It took time
to figure them out, to glean their stories, which was what they
wanted, but this was different. It felt like something hungering
for him.

Now about two miles from the wreckage and well into
the afternoon, he and the other men marched northward to
Blackthorne. Nobody spoke, until Tobias turned, alarmed at a
new touch upon his psyche back in the forest.

Sattler asked, "What is it?"

"I don't know," Tobias admitted. "I had a sudden feeling we
should go back."

"We can't go back," Michael said. "The day is passing fast. If
night falls before rescue, think of the trouble we'll have. It's out
of the question."

"No, I know that, of course. It's just . . ." Tobias let the thought
fall away.

Sattler pressed him. "What exactly did you feel?"

"I'm still feeling it. Under everything else, not on the surface. Something hiding from me."

Baffled, Sattler kept going. Tobias swallowed his worry and followed, for the first time unsure of himself. He hated being unclear in his head; it was, for him, the worst of feelings. Nervous, he hummed an old baroque tune to himself.

The trees behind them rattled in the wind, and everyone turned, startled.

Nothing was staring at them.

Nothing was there.

Tess sat with the other women in the dining car, fear for Tobias echoing in her, the cello phrases resounding in her mind now. She wondered if he could be hearing the same melody. She noticed the frost on the windows was slowly melting away.

"Is it letting up . . . ?" Elaine asked.

The storm did seem to be lessening in strength. As the snowfall eased, it was as if a veil was lifted . . . and they could see the burned-out skeleton of the old house in the forest. Ahead of the tall, imposing structure was a smaller home, partly restored and less derelict than the first. The physician had occupied the smaller building, and Tess shivered to remember the cold, deserted feeling there when she'd sought the telephone.

She looked at the others. "What . . . was that place, before the doctor took it?"

"It's the Mordecai settlement," Lucinda answered.

"It's where the so-called witches sought refuge," Elaine explained. "A doctor has just moved in there. He's a strange man, wants his peace and quiet, but he can't be cut off from people who might need him. He has plans to make the house more modern."

Tess's memory flashed back to the doctor's shaking body, his unnatural death-rattle. She wondered what could have brought this man to such a remote place. Had he somehow been called there, too? Long ago?

"Big place." Lucinda sighed. "A long time ago, the owner's daughter was going to make it a school for the blind. It ended up being built in Salem. But Blackthorne was always, you know, a haven for outcasts of one kind or another. When you put that many malcontents together you're going to have fire. And they did."

"Well, it's surely safe to say this town has seen a lot of very strange things," Tess said.

"That's putting it mildly. But I have hopes it could be a beautiful place one day. What can you say, every town has it secrets. And I'm starting to think of it as home already." Lucinda laughed. "We're not as famous as Salem. We just took the worst of their evils."

Again mist passed before the window like a veil.

"What do you know about the . . . witches?" asked Tess.

"They were running from the trials in Salem," said Elaine. "I think at first Blackthorne sympathized with them, didn't ask questions. But then after a few weeks came some suspicious deaths. Ritual deaths. No one was sure how they came about, but the bodies had been found in the fields, surrounded by a circle of blood. The same sorts of things that happened in Salem at the beginning. There were reports of a robed figure in the Salem woods, someone never captured, whom they called the First

Accused. They found bloody animals eviscerated and arranged with rocks alongside human hair and teeth, and once they found the jaw and entire flesh torn from the mouth of some poor girl, who'd been freshly dug up from a grave. For days the people heard the girl's voice, warning them to stay clear of the woods. And then this kind of chaos started up in Blackthorne."

Tess readily ate up their knowledge. "Do you know how that young couple figures into this?"

Lucinda broke in, leaning forward earnestly. "Well . . . when a young man named Wilhelm found his mother and father killed, blame fell to a woman the family had been fighting with over property lines; a lady called Widow Malgore. A bitter soul from the start. But her young daughter was very charming, they said. Very much so."

Tess settled herself back against the cold train window, and folded her arms in the chill, listening intently. "Tell me about the daughter."

"Well, all I know is, it starts back in Salem . . ." Lucinda smiled. "You see, this boy, Wilhelm, was from a German family. They were never quite welcome in town, and he fell in love with Abigail, the Malgore girl. Old lady Malgore always thought of him as a troublemaker, and when she became a widow, she got even more protective of her daughter. The boy even taught the girl to speak German, so her mother couldn't eavesdrop on them. But whatever problems the three of them had were interrupted by the Salem witch trials."

"My husband's a historian; we might as well make use of this." Elaine pulled out a book from a carrying bag. "But there's very little record of this. We know that Abigail's father died, and some said Wilhelm had a hand in that. Then later, it was Wilhelm's parents who ended up murdered, maybe by Missus Malgore, no one knows. Before long, the Malgore woman and her daughter Abigail were feared by all, and they ran from town to escape being killed.

"Got a picture here of the couple." She opened the book to a sketch: a young man and woman from an age long past. "Wilhelm and Abigail."

"She's beautiful," said Tess.

Elaine nodded. "They were beautiful together, so they say. As days rolled on, they had less interest in society and more and more in each other. But it's all hearsay really. Some old town letters said Wilhelm had a good mind, a love of books."

"He could read? Wasn't that unusual then?"

"Abigail helped him to read English, mostly using her father's beloved Bible, which he insisted his daughter learn, front to back. And then the real tensions came."

Elaine continued, "After her husband died, the widow Malgore came to truly hate the boy—and those she hated had a tendency to wind up with their guts cut out of them. She didn't get much opportunity, though. The Malgore women were to be locked up on the charge of witchcraft so they fled up here. But before they left, Abigail told Wilhelm where they were headed. Naturally the boy came after them and—well, he led the inquisitors right to them."

Elaine clucked her tongue. "He'd shown the witch-hunters the path as clearly as if he'd littered it with bread crumbs. The mob caught them by surprise, dragged the accused women screaming out into the street. It was said that one man pulled the young girl so hard by her hair, he pulled chunks of it out, and her head was bleeding at the roots . . ." She paused. "In the end, the boy was hanged here, too. For consorting with witches."

Tess pondered her words. "Was it the girl who left the curse on this place? Or the mother?" Tess asked.

"Nobody knows," said Elaine. "Some say it was the mother, some say the girl, but no one ever got much peace here. When a plague came to Blackthorne, they stacked the bodies like cord wood, and burned them as they left. The smell of burning flesh must have been just terrible, like a medieval village during the black death. Anyone who could walk got out, made a new life for themselves, and died peacefully beyond the woods, but there weren't many who lived. The town of Blackthorne was left empty as an old skull by the early 1700s. And it was pretty much forgotten."

Tess looked again at the sketch. The couple stared back blankly. "Was there anything they left unfinished? Something they wanted to do?" she wondered.

"They were young," said Lucinda. "Lot of living left to do. Some said they got married, but it's all come down to us by word of mouth."

"Well, we'd better get back," said Elaine, and as the ladies passed her, Tess lingered, transfixed by the sketch of the two young Puritans. "What are you trying to tell me . . . ?" she whispered. "What *is* it?"

But the mist, if it carried any souls within it, had departed.

And her feelings, reaching out, brought back only deadness and quiet.

CHAPTER TWENTY-ONE

〜※〜

Tobias stayed ahead of the two college men. Wilder was like a giant walking shadow behind them.

"*La strega, la strega.* Witch. Strange word. Do you know what a true witch is?" Wilder was saying. "It is a person who has grown so skilled in the black arts that she has captured a demon to do her bidding. It is human evil gone beyond the bounds of humanity, generous with its cruelties."

Wilder claimed to have seen "every form of evil" in his travels as a hired gun, and he accepted all talk of myth as fact and folk wisdom. He regretted leaving behind the witch-hunter's journal in the doctor's house, but claimed to remember every relevant bit of it.

"What are you talking about?" Tobias muttered.

"She was deformed by demonism, by drinking a devil's blood," Wilder went on. "Josiah Jurey said the Widow Malgore is a part of this place, able to move through it like the wind. She crosses the land in an instant; she can lift what lies before her without raising a finger; she is strong, but always needing new strength, and foul as a corpse. Black magic changed her into something no longer human."

"Of course she's no longer human. She's spirit," argued Tobias. "They're defined by want, spirits are. This creature, this witch, wants something. Maybe she just wants vengeance, or maybe she wants her husband back."

"I think not," Wilder rebuked him. "I think she was using magic against his wishes, long before the trials . . . roaming these woods, engaged in ritual so her crops would thrive where others failed, and to cause misfortune. She has been at this a long time."

Tobias scoffed. "Now you're just guessing aren't you? Unless your people know some voodoo that grants you insight. Exactly what nationality are you, anyway, Wilder?"

"I have the blood of many within me."

Tobias smiled. "Even you don't know."

"If I told you," said Wilder, "that I was born in Italy, lived for a time in Spain, and came to California to sell guns, which my father fashioned himself while teaching me Plato and Socrates at his knee, would you cease with your questions? Does it bring you satisfaction to know my brothers and I killed certain human targets for money, until I fell in love with one of my marks? Maybe I should tell you my grandmother made a spiced lamb that was as good as fine wine. Are you happy and pleased with this now as an answer?"

"I'm more confused than ever," Tobias said. "But never mind, Wilder, I don't need your history. I suppose it doesn't matter where you came from; we've all gotten what we came *for*, didn't we? Everyone headed to this ridiculous winter carnival is engaged in morbid curiosity. We're too comfortable in the modern world. There's no more wilderness, no more wolves, gentlemen."

Suddenly there was indeed the sound of a wolf, or perhaps some other animal, a heavy growling that seemed to come from everywhere, invisible, moving. . . .

Everyone stopped.

Even Tobias felt his pulse quicken.

But the growling slipped away as quickly as it had come.

Still, Tobias sensed something watching.

"What was it?" said Sattler.

"Who knows?" asked Michael. "It was just some animal."

"Oh, I'm certain it was," said Wilder, and his tone was most unbecoming.

Tobias clenched his jaw. "I don't like the progress we're making. Can we pick up the pace . . . ?"

They began moving faster. Tobias's eyes were stinging, he knew they were being followed. *Don't speak of it, don't acknowledge it.* It felt big, powerful, and he knew, right in his gut, that this was far stronger than he was.

He felt small and cold with an emotion he hadn't known since he was a child, and a bully three years older had battered his face, pushed him into the earth. And Tobias swung and swung but his punches were useless, like a bird's fragile beating wings in a man's hand. What he felt now was all of that and something else. The presence wanted something he couldn't quite figure out.

He was being stalked.

Behind him, deeper in the forest, hidden by a thicket of branches, a set of eyes watched him, cold, hunting, ready to strike.

And then the witch turned, and sniffed, alerted to the presence of two pale blue shapes, made of mist and frost, the spirits of Wilhelm and Abigail, high in the air, elusive forms that flew into the forest, fleeing her.

Malgore pursued.

How the hunt thrilled her.

CHAPTER TWENTY-TWO

From inside the train, Tess could see Annette outside, giving water to a man who'd been trapped, his legs pinned beneath an overturned car,. Tess could feel pulses of pain coming from him, a numb tingling in her own legs, but it was nothing compared to the man's fear. He was afraid of death, and knew it was near, and his sense of regret brought the taste of bile to her mouth. She was glad she was no closer to him.

As she watched the small crowds at the bonfires from the window, for an instant she thought she saw the train car behind them change, the air rippling and shuddering as if in a mirage. But she could not see clearly, for the windowpanes were somewhat warped. Annette had no reaction, so Tess thought it best to ignore what she might've seen. No sense in panicking everyone unnecessarily.

She turned to several blind boys huddled together for warmth near the piano. None were older than eleven years. Their eyes were dull, but they had that uncanny ability of those used to coping with other senses. As she stepped nearer to them they all turned at once, their gaze fell upon hers perfectly, and she felt her own sense of smell and touch—and especially hearing—pitch upward in intensity. Her vision stayed clear, but dimmed, like candlelight shuddering in a dark room.

"Have you ever had coffee?" she asked.

The smallest boy scowled. "Two times in the last hour."

His expression got a smile out of Tess. "We're just trying to keep you warm," she said, and noticed his discomfort. "I think you need to relieve yourself, am I correct? I'll tell you what. I have to give Miss Annette a break, so I'll go with you. You won't be alone."

The boy shook his head.

"Don't worry," scolded Tess. The boys' two female chaperones were clearly exhausted, and one had a knee injury.

But the little boy was not giving in. "I'm scared."

"Well, that's a very unique experience. Enjoy it. This is why they write ghost stories. Don't you just love that chill up your spine?" She grinned and took his hand. "It'll just take a second. I don't think you'd like being trapped in here in wet clothes."

He didn't smile. But he accepted her hand.

"If he don't want it, I could use some of that coffee m-m-myself." Carl hailed her with slurring speech. "If you please, ma'am." Tess handed him the cup, and he took it sadly. "People need me, and I can hardly keep myself w-walking straight. Plenty of good I do anybody. God hates the weak, don't He?"

The man was obviously drunk, and she wasn't sure what to say, so she led the blind boy onward.

Outside the parlor car, Tess opened the door and reached for his hand to help him down. "You're perfectly safe here."

He let go of her, still resistant. He seemed to recognize the unknown danger in the woods, leaving Tess to consider if he had a supernatural awareness. The boy shivered. Despite this, he came out of the train car, stepped to the ground.

Tess was fighting her own urge to hide inside, but if he was strong enough to face the fear, so could she. As she moved to take his arm, *she was sucked back into the train.* The door slammed.

She was in shock. She couldn't see the boy outside; he must have fallen.

The door was jammed.

Through the window, Tess saw Annette approaching the boy and behind her, the air rippling again. Tess was sure she saw it this time, but then something else caught her eye, a white motion in the wilderness.

It was a skeletal figure, a woman, hunching down beside a tree. The woman, or whatever it truly was, reached into its own chest, and pulled loose a white pulse of light from its innards.

It opened its hand, and the light flashed, and vanished; the train car shook and rattled from its energy, as Tess realized what the woman was.

The witch—the Beast—had come for them.

A mist outside the car had spread quickly to swallow everything in sight, and Tess saw the witch dart away into the forest.

All of this happened with great speed, and Tess became aware that the other train cars were being rocked and pummeled, as the witch's power spread malevolently through the clearing.

Inside the parlor car, Tess tried to get free to help the blind boy, but the door was unmovable. She yelled, but her voice was drowned out.

Tess fell against the door and could see from the window that the blind boy was crawling about in terror on the snowbank. He suddenly reversed, and dived under the train, but—astonished—Tess could see him yanked out again in a thrashing of snow. Something was dragging him.

He screamed, and his face was lit up for a fraction of a second by vivid lightning. Annette rushed toward him, but was thrown back onto the ground.

The boy clutched his head, and suddenly he seized up, shaking horribly. It was as if ghostly, skinless hands had burst *from his head* and were clutched over his mouth.

Tess could see dimly the hands of the witch in the forest, mimicking this action, controlling it. The boy grabbed for his face—a sight so dreamlike and shocking Tess had to look away.

She could see Annette on the ground, trying to get to the child. But something was pulling her deeper into the snow, half burying her, as she screamed in terror.

White light was crackling around Annette. Coils of electricity flashed and vanished as the witch's magic gripped her, tugging her downward.

The power of the wretch was everywhere at once.

There were forty or fifty people on the snow, and many of them started forward to help the boy, who was being dragged away as if by invisible chains. Tess instinctively knew it was a trap, but was powerless to stop them from rushing to him.

Malgore moved in.

Charging in a white blur, the witch-creature slashed down survivors, wielding a long crescent-shaped knife.

The beastlike wretch was only glimpsed by Tess as the travelers shrieked, trying to make their way back into the train cars. They could not get the doors open. Tess screamed. They were being raked down, stabbed, pulled back into the snow. Someone would go down, then someone else—and a white skeletal hand would flash out of the mist and snow, reaching from behind the crowd to kill, to pull down, to slash at will.

Tess couldn't breathe. She still struggled with the door but it was locked hopelessly.

Outside, Annette was pulled back farther, into the woods.

The man trapped under the train could not see behind him but Tess heard his screams of horror. The train was still shaking brutally. More screams tore the air from survivors inside.

Tess was yelling with them, to Annette, to anyone, just wanting to scream the Thing away, to fight, and it was all she had, her voice, as the sizzling flashes of light that surrounded Annette tossed her aside. Tess's stomach dropped. The wretch was moving on. She had attracted it.

It was coming for her, now.

Inside the parlor car, a bluish mist began oozing from the ceiling.

Everyone screamed. The blind boys cried out and buried their heads. The mist was slipping in through cracks in the windows and under the doors, relentlessly.

Strangely, as it moved over them, Tess had a clear feeling that the mist was a *solace*. The haze was a spirit, and it was running from the witch, terrorized. Distinct from the crackling white power emanating from the wretch, the mist was of a blue twilight hue. It filled Tess with a state of wonder.

But Malgore had located this new spirit. The wretch sent its hand forward, shocking the car with pulses of pale light.

Tess turned. All around her people's faces were lit up briefly— she saw skulls partially revealed and filled with light, faces halved into skeleton and flesh, bones visible as if burned from inside.

Tess saw one blind boy screaming, hysterical, saying, "I want to see—I want to see—"

And another screeching, "No—no—no—"

The power of the witch was searching inside the car; Tess knew it was searching for the spirit. There was nowhere to run. She turned and saw the indigo mist forming into a human shape beside her.

It was a Puritan girl—sixteen years old, maybe less—kneeling beside her, staring ahead at the bright pulses of light, as terrified of the witch's power as anyone. The spectre looked into Tess with eyes of sorrow and desperate need, but she could not speak: She shouted, but no voice came forth.

Tess watched as the girl broke into a sea-colored mist that flooded toward Tess, who screamed, joining her shrieking with the others'.

CHAPTER TWENTY-THREE

The blue mist reached into Tess. She stared horror-struck as it passed through her, leaving part of her body aglow.

The mist was moving like a snake inside her, splintering into many, slithering in her intestines, her stomach shuddering, her muscles weakened.

Mist-tendrils whipped upward, stabbing into her head.

Her eyes shut, for an instant Tess experienced a flood of emotions and then felt nothing but cold. Her brain felt punctured as if by a sword of ice.

She saw a rapid scattering of pictures in her mind's eye: scarecrows, hands, a church, the train, as she detached from the reality before her.

In warm yellow light she awoke. She was in a different train car, snow covering the windows. Everything was moving strangely, fast and then slow. She was staring at many well-dressed men and women, in clothes such as her parents might have worn. They were being thrown against the walls.

A woman was screeching, "GET THE CHILDREN OUT!!"

And a ghostly female voice hissed an icy sound, "We do not want to hurt—"

And Tess knew she was seeing the story Lucinda had told her of the buried train, only it was not a story but the truth seen through someone's eyes.

Someone who had been there.

The Puritan girl was trying to speak in the only way she knew how, through dreams and images. This was a warning, a message about her mother, the true witch, and Tess knew this as if it were her own knowledge. Then everything before Tess vanished.

She found herself now in yet another dark passenger car, with a group of children. They had barricaded the door, and their hearts were filled with terror. As if in a dream, an older girl of nine or ten years looked at Tess, saying "She wants us dead, she wants us all dead . . .

"She would feed on us," intoned the girl, in a slow, empty voice. "Malgore, they say she chews you open and feeds on your bones while you live . . . keeps you alive to feel the pain . . . and takes your bones to use in her magic . . .

"*Your spine,*" she whispered, "*she rips your spine out and curls it round her bed—*"

"No . . . ," murmured Tess.

The girl nodded. "In Blackthorne, men killed themselves before she could get to them. They did not want to die at her hands. We shall all be murdered here, Lord deliver us. . . ."

Tess knew. The little girl had never said such words. It was the ghost speaking as directly as it could. Dream was blending with memory.

Then the vision was gone.

★ ★ ★

She awoke feeling dazed, the influence of the ghost still clinging.

Outside in the field beyond, Tess saw the lost blind boy, his face normal and restored, alive but wracked with fear. She shot a glance to Annette, who was pulling herself up, safe, free of the snowy ground that had held her like a living thing.

The witch's power was weakening.

Her abilities are not endless, thought Tess with relief.

She tried the door. It gave.

She smashed her way into the snow, Abigail's spirit still inside her. Shouts came from the train behind her and she glanced back wildly, seeing figures in the whitened windows. She battered at her chest, to drive out the thing within, and fell to the icy earth.

A force poured out of Tess, rippling the air, and shaping itself into the figure of a young Puritan woman. The bottom of her face was gone, mere vapor, and then all of her fell away into glimmering ether.

Still searching for her, the witch pursued, leaping from the train roof, limping grotesquely. Tess saw her suddenly stop as she came upon the body of Josiah Jurey in the snow.

Malgore saw the cross and other amulets upon it. She hissed, crunching his ankle in her claws, and dragged the witch-hunter off into the woods.

Tess watched the ghostly feminine form of Abigail, a flowing curtain of blurring waves in the air, and below that, the witch striding off, a swift shape in the snow, limping, moving unnaturally, dragging its dead prize.

★ ★ ★

Long after Tess was free of the encounter, Malgore continued to pursue the misty cerulean form of Abigail. With its animal mind, the witch knew the spirit desperately wanted to be followed. The bait would not be taken. Abigail desired nothing more than to draw Malgore away—but the witch would not be deceived into leaving her human prey out there in the forest ahead.

The widow dropped Josiah Jurey, leaving him like a hunter's kill. She hissed and after a moment, something huge crackled in the brush in response. Malgore gave a satisfied sigh, motioning her servant closer.

Now she would hunt the men properly.

CHAPTER TWENTY-FOUR

❧

Michael and Sattler tried to keep pace with Tobias as the pale daylight crawled on toward three, then four o'clock. The woods were as still and quiet as the day of creation. Tobias shook himself out of a daze.

Wilder was saying, "These woods were feared by the Indians long before any Salem witches came into it. That's what the old man on the train said. He said the creature came to gain strength from the power emanating here."

For just an instant, Tobias saw shapes in the dim, snow-shrouded forest, hundreds of them, *people* in ragged old-fashioned dress.

"Do you . . . sense something?" Sattler asked.

"I sense nothing but happiness and dandelions out there, waiting to be reborn." Tobias kept going, visibly nervous. Were the dead railworkers? The deceased from Blackthorne, the burned bodies from the plague?

"Come now. What did you see?" Sattler was used to his bleak humor by now.

Shrugging him off, Tobias treaded onward. *Many died here.* He was thinking. *They're tied to the place, but put it out of your mind— they're not the ones to fear. There's something else out there.*

The other men were calling for him to slow down, but Tobias was slogging on. "We have people counting on us. I'm sure that's as new a feeling for you as it is for me, but that's that."

And then there was silence, a hole of sound where the young men should have been.

Tobias turned. The others were gone. The forest had been swallowed by the smoky blue and white mist. His heart was pumping hard.

"Sattler?"

He heard their voices calling, distant.

Michael: "Where are you—?"

Sattler: "What in God's name happened?"

Staring at the wall of fog, Tobias turned, listening, the voices moving around him. . . .

"Can anybody hear me?" called Sattler.

His voice trailed off, as did Michael's. There was no sign of Wilder at all. Tobias saw the haze in the forest growing, reaching toward him.

He gave a quick prayer. In an instant the mist surrounded him.

Tobias stumbled around in the gloom, fearful, listening, lost in the snow-painted trees, trying to be calm. "Are you here . . . ?"

But there was no answer.

Suddenly Tobias heard a low growl at his side. He could see nothing in the drifting, cloudlike masses. Then a more disturbing sound came from directly in front of him.

It was a savage howl, a murderous cat-kill screech carved out of the quiet, and out of the mist before him, Tobias saw Michael thrown to the ground, a rageful white creature pouncing upon him with incredible fury. Tobias stared in shock.

He stumbled back, away from the white beast—what was surely a witch—but Tobias was so stunned he could not find the word in his head. The thing ripped into Michael's flesh, his arm, his chest, the college boy's fingers were snapped by the creature's jaws. Michael's head slammed backward, and he fell unconscious.

The creature looked up, saw Tobias, and dropped its attack on Michael. Instead, it began slowly, inexorably, striding toward him.

For a moment Tobias could only stare.

He thought he saw the shadow of a wolf behind the witch, moving toward Michael. But the mist seemed to shuttle the four-legged creature away, and Tobias had no more courage to watch.

He turned to run, but Malgore leaped for him, as he felt a rush of air from behind. His head met the ground hard, the witch's brutal strength pushing down upon him.

He looked up, gasping. The Thing was astonishing. To call it a "witch" was to stretch the definition. It was a beast, a horror, its skull stretched and deformed, its feminine face tightly narrow and extremely thin, barely covered in white skin and crowned with a long mane. A skeletal woman with small, bright eyes loomed over him.

It opened its huge jaws, rising back for a final, joyous strike of death—

But Wilder rushed out behind it, firing his pistol. The witch was struck, but turning, it flew at Wilder and pinned him to a tree.

Tobias was staring in a near stupor when he felt a grasping at his arms. Out of nowhere a misty form tugged him back, lifting him high off the ground, pulling him up into a tree to safety.

He could scarcely see what had saved him. Tobias glanced at the shape, which had the vague look of a man in Puritan clothes, but it was blurred, subtle, becoming mist almost as soon as Tobias cast his eyes upon it.

Below him, Malgore slammed Wilder against the tree again and again, his enormous frame struggling. Behind the creature, a second billowing presence, this one female, was soaring away, and the witch turned to it, hissing.

The witch gave chase, releasing Wilder to choke upon the ground.

High in the tree, Tobias searched for the apparition that had saved him, and then had faded as if worn out. Suddenly it made itself known as a coil of indigo vapor that whipped around the tree, becoming the slightest outline of a human form, the ghost soaring into Tobias, its hand touching his forehead. Tobias felt electrified, as the spirit broke through his skin, firing each nerve in his brain. He felt as if a gauzy substance, a curtain, were brushing upon the interior of his head. He took in a rapid flash of images: scarecrows, Salem, the train, axes, torches . . .

Tobias Goodraven felt his identity merge with another.

CHAPTER TWENTY-FIVE

A nd then he was somewhere else. Tobias stood before a set of open church doors. Within the church, staring out, were the faces of angry men. Their gaze was so unkind, their appearance so disturbing, their bones so severe and sharp that Tobias felt it hard to withstand the sight of them. He had a sense somehow that he would be forced to enter this place and confront them.

But gradually light engulfed them, and he found himself standing in a crowd in front of a gallows. He was seeing the Puritan witches being hanged: A young man, a young woman, and her mother. The crowd was shouting. The bodies fell, one after the other, jerking, writhing on the ropes.

A flash engaged Tobias's vision, the moment passed, and the bodies were dragged away by the mob. The old woman was thrown down a hill, and left to lie in a ravine. As the crowd left, Tobias stared down at her from the top of the hill. She was twitching, her emerald-white eyes upon his, otherworldly. She was alive.

Tobias knew what she was. In an instant, he became aware that the woman was once a living person, vicious, brutish, that she was now cheating death. She had only seemed to die, had worked a dark and terrible blood magic, feeding on a force in the forest older than anything known.

Her wounds dripped from where the crowd had stoned her, and the stringy tatters she wore were clotted with crimson. She arose, thin muscles pulling her body out of the dead creek, and moved, sluglike, her mouth close to the dirt, her eyes smoldering in fury. Dragging herself up the hill, she was pure determination. Her white hair had fallen back from her high, withered forehead, and with the taut flesh of her face exposed, she was the equal of any creature in hell, ready for new life, power, and vengeance.

Tobias was seeing the Malgore witch being born, a living thing, but no longer human.

He was being given a history of horrors, as the ghost of the Puritan boy was showing him events of two hundred years ago in a bright, clear, unflinching vision. And the mystery that turned inside Tobias was, *Why?* What did the spirit want from him?

Tess lay on the snowy ground where she had fled, her eyes clenched shut as she heard the train metal stop rattling somewhere behind her. She opened her eyes. Her body was hers again.

The spirit had gone.

It went to find strength, Tess thought, to gather energy for another strike. There was time yet to prepare.

Tess stood up and moved across the snow to the train. Underneath her fear, she felt, at the back of her mind, a strange, buried *envy*. The spirits could move together, pass into each other; know one another with unimaginable intimacy. Their secrets, their history, their shared tragedy would be fully experienced by both together.

Their feelings could never be hidden or ambiguous.

She saw Annette just ahead, and moved toward her. "They're being kept apart," Tess whispered to her.

"What?"

"I felt their isolation . . ." She knew Tobias would've seen it had he been here.

"I don't understand."

"The ghosts of Salem," said Tess, thinking aloud, her voice shaking. "There was something they wanted me to *feel*. It's the widow Malgore. . . . she's trying to keep them apart. She's killed or she's driven out everyone they've come near, everyone . . . to keep them apart."

"Who?"

"Wilhelm. Abigail. They've been trying to reach us . . ."

"Reach us for what, Tess?"

Tess gazed at her, unsure. The question hung in the air.

There was something very touching about Annette, looking so helpful. Tess cursed herself for listening to Tobias, for letting him desert her. *Where in God's name was he?*

Tobias awoke in the snow. He had fallen from the tree and survived, but Wilder was gone. Not a soul was visible in the woods. Except the one leaving him. Light and vapor fled his body, soaring away in the snowfall.

It was a man's form, in Puritan hat and cloak, but hardly there, like a rippling silk, blown away, growing even more indistinct, just silvery light fading and soon lost in the trees.

It joined with the second spirit-shape, the ghost of Abigail, and the two vanished into the distant air.

And then from the other direction, out of the mist and trees, an emaciated woman with alabaster skin was coming forth, wrapped in animal pelts, and she was raised up, high, and Tobias saw that she was riding an immense black creature.

Tobias looked upon it with total incredulity.

It appeared to be a great black jaguar, with massive muscles and odd lumps of flesh beneath its slick hide. Its slightly misshapen head was marred by tumorous clumps and growths covered in dark fur, and two small sharpened horns. It stepped over to Tobias, its fangs bared. The woman leaned down and hissed savagely. She grinned, showing ragged teeth made of thorns, and a bony, almost-feline face, like that of her steed.

Widow Malgore had returned.

She had donned the gear of hunting, as her sick mind saw fit, and she was enjoying the pleasures of the chase.

She kicked at the jaguar—who proceeded to dive into Tobias's chest, lifting him. Tobias wheezed painfully as he was flung around, writhing, and he could see the snout and jaws of the animal on his chest, clutching his clothes. He was trapped in those strong jaws, hanging by the loose clothing at his midsection as if he were held in a sack. His feelings were of detached horror—*how very strange, these jaws have hold of me . . .*

"Tobias!"

It was Wilder, rising from behind a tree, injured but fighting, firing his pistols. The huge jaguar was struck in the middle, crying out; it dropped Tobias, leaving him gasping. Widow Malgore stabbed the cat with a small pitchfork, and the monstrous animal galloped away in extraordinary leaps, carrying her into the mist.

Wilder went to Tobias, lifting his head. "Are you all right?"

"Exceptional."

"The others?"

Tobias shook his head, not knowing.

"*Diàvolo*. It was her demon, wasn't it? In thrall to her . . . ," Wilder asked, quoting the nursery rhyme. "'Old Widow Malgore, kept a devil slave . . .'?"

Tobias couldn't answer that, but told him of the spirit-vision he'd received from Wilhelm, and his discovery: "She's alive. She can be killed."

The foreigner scoffed. "I always believed it. It was never in doubt, Goodraven. That's what this is for." He set down the witch's dagger in the snow. "But you wouldn't listen. I suppose we have to learn things for ourselves, don't we?"

"This is proof, don't you understand? The spirit is helping us; I saw the mother survive the gallows with my own eyes."

He wasn't sure Wilder was even listening to him; the man was examining Tobias's injuries. "Your wound's not deep, *signore*, you'll be all right," Wilder said, "and she'll need time to draw strength. We need to keep moving. I can protect you."

"That's no longer convincing."

Wilder scowled. "I shall tear the head off the wretch and crush her skull. . . ."

Without warning Malgore flew from the mist and leaped upon him. His eyes went wide. He'd been stabbed in the back.

Tobias gaped in horror as the huge man's face imploded, sucked inward.

The witch pulled back, floating above, carrying Wilder's spine in her claws.

His skeleton had separated from his body.

Wilder's skin flagged to the ground, bloodless, in a heap. The witch dropped his bones to the snow, and turned, flying back into the mist, her strength depleted.

It was an instant and nothing more.

Tobias stood stunned before the grisly heap of skin and bones. The man was dead.

Wilder was dead.

The wretch was gone, a retreat made clear by a long, terrible silence in the woods.

Tobias stumbled away, and stared into the white void.

After a time, Tobias retrieved Malgore's dagger and pocketed it, though he could hardly imagine putting it to use. He slumped into the snow, placing his back against a tree, shivering, fighting to keep his brain working.

Eventually, he became aware that Sattler was running toward him from ahead in the woods. "WE CAN SEE THE TOWN ...," he was yelling.

Saying nothing, Tobias remained in a daze, as Sattler got closer. He was shuddering uncontrollably. There was little hope of getting through this now. Wilder had been the most capable of them, and they had lost his protection. The spirits could not keep Tobias safe and Malgore was out here, somewhere alongside them in the forest. They would be killed for certain.

"What happened?"

Tobias was not speaking, his thoughts running wild. Whatever it was the Puritan wanted him to know, the wretch did not want him to hear it. He had only part of a message.

"It's an endless feud . . . between them . . . and I don't know how to end it," Tobias uttered quietly, not sure if his words were even audible. "I'm going to die here no matter what."

Sattler stared at him in shock.

But Tobias knew, it was the truth.

CHAPTER TWENTY-SIX

T ess and Annette were looking for the missing blind boy away from the train, deeper into the woods. Annette had witnessed the spirit ripping away from Tess's body, and was extremely disturbed. "Are you sure you're all right?" she asked Tess.

Tess said nothing.

She felt as closed-in as if she'd been in a coffin, and she could scarcely find the air to breathe. Her throat tightened. Her skin, even the skin of her eyelids, felt taut. She felt exposed and so very far from help.

"Say something calming," Tess asked her. "Tell me about the children you want to teach."

Annette searched for words. "When all this is past, I'll bring you to the blind children's school. And you can see what I have done. I think the key to their lives is going to be music."

"Music?"

"A blind child who is trained in music is useful. He or she could be employed playing piano or harp at a hotel or such. Imagine being free of charity. I have in mind that there could be an orchestra of them, world-class, all of them living quite well on their earnings."

It wasn't an unintelligent plan, Tess thought. It was something that could truly change lives. The surprise of it distracted Tess; she was ashamed that she'd dismissed Annette as petty and small-minded.

"I know the blind school is here to make those rich investors feel better about their greed, but it's still a good thing," Annette added. "Those children will benefit."

Unthinkingly, Tess said, "I'm sorry."

"Sorry? For what?"

"For thinking so little of you. For thinking you were keeping secrets from your fiancée with Michael—"

"Michael's feelings are not to be discussed," Annette said, incensed. "He isn't the way you might think. He's the only one who knows I can't have children, and that's because Sattler might not marry me if he found out."

Tess felt even worse. "I didn't know that."

"You can't know everything, Tess, whatever you may think. Judge less and help more."

This might have been like a hard slap to the face on a different day, but Tess was still absorbing the very fact of being alive. That relief passed quickly, though: a crackling in the nearby trees silenced the girls.

Then for a long moment, there was no sound at all.

"This Thing, this witch has such power," Annette whispered. "She seems to cross space with mere thought. . . ."

But Tess had no reply. Her eyes were fixed forward in absolute terror.

The fog was thickening about her. She couldn't see.

It had to be the spirit out here. This was how she traveled. But not alone; Tess could now hear people getting closer, calling for help, the muted cries of survivors.

"It's . . . trying to get inside us . . . ," Annette said. "The spirit tries to hide within . . ."

"It's desperate," Tess tried to explain. "It wants to reach us."

Annette looked tearful. "Tess . . . I think it's inside *me* . . ." The mist seemed to come from behind and melt into her, as her veins and her bones glowed inside her, now her abdomen, *burning* with light, vaguely blue as the mist moved down her. Then suddenly the witch was there, throwing Annette's body back furiously against a tree.

Nauseated, Tess heard bones breaking. And for the moment the light burned within the girl, Tess could see her skeleton, and another skeleton coming against it as she saw the two merge.

The witch's claws had reached deep inside the young woman, trying to grasp the blue skeletal spirit inside her, pulling it loose.

For an instant, Malgore appeared to be holding a shimmering blue veil of light, Abigail's very soul, but the spirit slipped out and escaped her claws, gliding free. Furious, the witch pursued the spectral entity, and the two passed into the snow and mist and could no longer be seen.

Annette's lifeless body collapsed to the ground.

In terror, Tess ran the other way into the forest. Heart pounding, she came upon a spray of broken dolls—battered china girls with rouged faces and black pupils staring upward—lying in the snow. They were littered around the dead body of the thin woman, who still clutched several of her precious recovered toys.

Tess realized that anyone the spirit tried to reach, the witch destroyed immediately, and with astonishing savagery. Over and over, Malgore had wrecked her daughter's only voice to the world. . . .

Exhausted, Tess fell against a tree, listening, watching—as a boy ran past, his hands feeling blindly before him. Ahead of him, Malgore glided out of the frost, a flying, grinning thing dripping with ice, in animal hood and robes.

Malgore blocked the panicked child. The boy stopped, out of space. The witch sniffed at him. She reached out a skeletal finger, stopping at the youngster's eyes. A look of disgust crossed her visage, and the wretch shoved the boy to the ground, dispensing with him.

Is he no amusement for you, thought Tess, *unless he's bait for others?*

Malgore stalked away into the woods, and the downed boy slowly turned as if aware of Tess.

He panted, whispering, "Are you . . . alive . . . ?"

Unable to speak, she took his hands, put them to her face, and nodded.

The two of them stayed hidden, clutched together against the tree a long time. When finally the woods grew completely quiet, Tess eased out and peered around the tree, but little could be seen through the mist. Fallen bodies could be dimly made out, but she had no way of knowing for sure who had been lost.

She slipped back to the tree.

"I don't hear it anymore," whispered the boy.

"No."

A little more time passed, and Tess found the courage to move from hiding. Suddenly something lunged at her from the other side.

Carl's body slumped to the ground.

Drunk as he was, he'd gone out to help the others. She shouted as he fell, his corpse plunging into the snow.

Terrified she'd given her location away, she stood quiet, looking around. She snatched up the blind boy's hand and ran amid the trees, toward the train for shelter.

As they got closer, shadows in the car windows moved; people awake now, talking.

Tess stopped just before entering, *feeling* exactly what was happening inside with the survivors. "They're fighting. They're going to turn against each other."

She gripped the boy's hand tighter, filled with dread.

At a small hill, Michael stood waiting as Tobias and Sattler caught up to him. Coughing now, with a bloodied arm, he seemed weaker than ever. Tobias looked at him and thought, Some people, even if they're timid, pull themselves together in a crisis and find the guts to go on. Not so with this one.

Sattler begrudgingly helped Michael rebandage his arm.

Looking inward, Tobias found that he had been more capable than he'd imagined. If only his mind would work as well as his body; the clues had been laid before him, but they did not quite fit properly. The dead couple; the doctor; the flashing of images; surviving the accident by some aid: what was the sum total of all these parts?

They rested, catching their breath. It was quiet. No one wanted to discuss their chances. Tobias yearned for the cleverness of Tess. The cold was seeping into him. Strange, how in a wintery place, thoughts seem to slow.

"I don't know what it is I have to do," he said, still in a numbed state of mind, his shock wearing upon him even now.

Sattler stared.

"They've been separated. They can't touch. But I don't know how to bring them together," he went on. "They can't expect me to kill Malgore, I wouldn't know . . ."

"I don't think I understand you."

Tobias looked at him, lost. "These things are asking me to do something and I don't know what. Bring them their earthly possessions? Is that what they want?"

"You mean the box we took, with their wedding rings?"

Tobias was too deep in thought to answer, so Sattler looked at Michael for a response. "What is he talking about?"

Tobias pulled himself out of his daze and patiently explained, "These objects take on tremendous significance in the dead mind. The spirits may gain strength from them . . . possibly . . . "

"Strength for what?" asked Sattler.

"To kill the witch."

Baffled, Sattler and Michael looked at him as if he were insane.

"We have to bring the spirits their possessions," Tobias said emphatically. "So they can rid us of that thing. Are you listening to a word I've said?"

"I think we've all been out here too long . . . ," said Michael.

He'd lost consciousness during the attack, and wasn't at all sure what he had seen. Only some beast in the fog, possibly a wolf, he told himself, something that he could accept as real. "Let's just get on to safety now . . ."

And he looked up, carrying everyone's gaze to the winter village ahead of them on the hill. The winter carnival awaited.

CHAPTER TWENTY-SEVEN

O utside, still terribly shaken, Tess and the young boy were gathered by the overcrowded parlor car. They found everyone, inside and out, wrapped in noisy debate, terrified, unsure as to what had truly happened.

Stuck outside with the bulk of the crowd, Tess watched in a dazed and ironically unhurried state of mind. Men yelled. Women shook their heads. People pointed, gestured. She forced herself to focus again.

The men had moved the bodies taken by the latest attack out onto the snow, but the grisly work had taken its toll on everyone. It was late afternoon now, and night would be hurtling toward them soon.

"This is going to keep happening until we are dead or we all lose our minds," said one man.

Someone was muttering to himself, "Why did it only take some of us . . . ?"

Another man outside shouted, "We want on there—we want in the train—"

"There isn't enough room for all of you!"

"Then you come out and *make* room—"

"Wait a minute." Tess raised her hands, facing the train car. "You can't leave all of us out here in the cold."

Alan, whom Tess remembered was a Navy man, looked at her sharply from the train, a rush of panic coming off him. "Only two of the cars offer real protection. What would you have us do?"

"There has to be a fair way to divide these cars," Tess answered. "We cannot do this. We cannot lose all civility," she cried.

"Look, now," Alan growled, "no one is coming for us. I don't know what happened to those young men, but someone is going to have to go after them and get us help."

No one in the crowd called for violence, but their faces clearly favored the idea. Tess felt their desperation. She faced Alan. "Whatever's out here is getting closer and it is getting angrier. We have to construct a barricade."

"Barricade won't do it," yelled an angry man, and he lunged to pull Alan off the train. But Alan kicked him back, and slammed the train door shut as the crowd surged forward, begging for entry.

Tess cried out for calm, "We can't do this— Stop—" but her voice was drowned out by the crowd. She escaped the mob, which hammered at the train everywhere, and managed to get to Ned, who was scarcely able to speak after the loss of Annette.

"I can't handle this alone," she told him.

He looked at her with sympathy. "You don't have to. I'm with you."

Indignantly, Tess looked back at the train. "They're not going to help us."

Their world was divided between those on the train and those left out. None of them were safe, but she felt betrayed, watching

Alan and the others, locked behind the car windows. They looked back at her with only worry in their eyes. They were used to little hardships, perhaps, but nothing worse.

It felt like the woods behind her were moving in, the earth slipping under her feet, a near vertigo clouding her mind. *What insanity ever to travel here.* Trying to catch her breath, Tess saw Lucinda moving out of the crowd.

"Where is Elaine?" the Southern woman asked. "I can't find her. I think she's gone."

"Lucinda," Tess said, vacantly, as though in a daydream.

"Tess, wake up. We need you. We need to know who's left. What are we going to do for the wounded?"

There were still badly injured survivors in damaged train cars, far from the main body of the train. They were the ones who couldn't be moved at all, and there was no one to help tend to them.

Just over half the original survivors remained alive now, Tess realized in shock. Perhaps a hundred people left in all? From where she stood, she counted perhaps two score, outside with her, unprotected. It had been a massacre.

She pulled in a bracing breath of cold air, thinking she'd rather run away than face all that needed to be done. She had a confused longing to turn into the forest and leave it all behind no matter what the risk, to leave the people here as bait for the witch, and escape in the chaos.

It seemed now that a riot was erupting. Ned pulled her and Lucinda away from the growing mob trying to break into the train. Rocks were being thrown. There was nothing Tess could do;

it was like a dream. She could only stand there with her newfound allies and watch everything fall apart.

The wind picked up and ice scraped over the snow. No one was sure if this somehow meant Malgore was near, but Tess felt nothing stirring her deep senses.

"It's getting colder. I'll bet we don't have much more than an hour left of light," Ned said.

They huddled together. Tess felt the softness of his wide stomach against her elbows, as she held her arms clutched against her chest. He looked down at her worriedly. "What do we do? How long can we withstand this?"

"I don't know." Tess sighed.

Lucinda watched the crowd silently, ashen, unable to say anything.

"I feel like the cold is coming from my insides out," Ned uttered thoughtfully.

Tess was now distracted, for the angered crowd was breaking up; strangely enough, she was seeing people moving away, toward the icy lake. Her eyes began watering, tears coming to them in some premonition of some great sadness she couldn't make clear in her head. Suddenly, there was a shattering sound of ice. People yelled, pointing.

Then the cause of her strange pain became more clear. Out of the frozen lake the buried train car was emerging, bursting out of the ice with a kind of electrical crackle. There was a sudden billowing of energy from the panicked survivors all around Tess. And they started moving in the direction of the lake, leaving the train to help. Tess trailed them, feeling sure that it was wrong to go.

And then she stopped. Knowing. The others rushed forward, while Tess stood watching, afraid, as they closed in, and the watery door fell open.

The rescuers suddenly slowed, confusion played out on their faces, struck by disbelief and horror. The storm was building, snow whipping around them—as Tess hung back, fearing what it was in the car.

"What is it? What do you see?" She had to scream to be heard over the wind.

Behind her, Lucinda was yelling; the weather, the elements, raging around her even more fiercely now . . . as the men up ahead saw into the train car. And they were looking at their own bodies. Leo and Alan and all of them, dead, looking at their own remains, and Tess saw it happening, saw it all so slowly unfolding and now the snow came charging across the angry landscape, and they began to vanish with it, swept away by the wind.

Tess turned back, looking to the train.

Lucinda was calling out, "Oh God . . ."

She and others stood staring back at Tess—and then slowly faded away. Tess saw them vanish from afar, leaving the train a solitary darkness, a collection of black objects in a long broken line. Snow swept across the landscape, wiping it clean of life. . . .

They were gone.

Tess felt her heart trembling. Her breath held half-started prayers; she could not bring herself to move, and everything in her rejected what she was seeing. These people were not dead. It was impossible. She had seen them, held their hands, spoken to them, for hours. She needed them, she could not get through this alone. She looked around in terror, abandoned.

Ned was stumbling toward her, his face pained and disoriented.

The body he was carrying was his own.

The snow lashed around him and behind it his dark shape vanished, the body collapsing to the ground. Then he was gone.

Tess was in absolute shock. *God help me. This is real. This is real. . . .*

Somewhere behind her, a boy stood terrified in the snow in front of the train, unable to move. "THEY'RE GONE—HELP ME—SOMEONE!" His screams were being eaten by the winds.

And Tess truly comprehended. They were no longer alive, but they could not accept it; they had lived on, believing themselves to be survivors. They had warped nature around them, the signs had been there. Everyone around her was fading away in the dim light of winter. They had been killed by the wreck, the storm, or the Thing itself; but they had been killed one by one. They were gone, all of them.

The snow charged across the land, and the trees, and the lake, and took every last ghostly breath from the place, erased the other travelers from existence, for they now knew what they were.

Phantoms.

CHAPTER TWENTY-EIGHT

ess tried to regain her strength, hearing the screams of children. Only the boys of the blind school remained alive. Why they had been spared she didn't know, but they had no one left to help them except for her. Their chaperones were dead.

And the others were gone as well, all of them, reclaimed by the white woods that had let them live on for a time after death; the mysterious, swirling power of the place taking them in at last, making their souls part of the snow and the mist, twisting their lives into the gnarled roots of the trees, the fingerlike branches, the poisonous brambles and old thorns in the winterscape, into the depths of the lake. Tess knew the essence of who they were had joined with the woods, to feed, and be fed upon.

Whatever had fed the longest in the woods, the strongest of its evils, had chosen now to move in. Malgore was coming back.

Tess could feel her hatred now.

With nowhere else to run, Tess clambered back into the parlor car, coming face-to-face with one of the blind boys. They were all huddling together inside.

"Who's there?" said the child, his voice a whimper.

Tess could hardly find words. "They didn't know . . . They'd lost their lives . . . She brought the car up. They . . ."

"Who's left? Who's left?"

Tess shook her head. "She wanted them to know . . . We're hers . . . We're all—"

Suddenly Malgore leaped into sight at the door.

The creature rushed forward, her jaws missing Tess's face as she ran, but tearing a tiny piece of flesh from her ear in a small spray of blood. Tess, screaming, crawled away fast, as Malgore reached, groping, her claw slipping from Tess's boots.

The children ran for the back of the train, squealing, almost fighting each other. Tess kicked, and the creature fell back, clinging to the door, grinning wildly. Screaming, Tess turned away, and when she looked back . . .

The wretch was gone. The door slammed shut.

Tess panted for air. Malgore had seemed light and weakened, her bones birdlike. Was she drained of strength now?

Then, from the window, Tess could see Malgore's eyes.

What she saw next were the eyes disappearing and a long panicked moment passed. When Malgore returned, she lifted a burning torch from the bonfire outside—and the window was covered in flames.

The witch glared, fire reflected in her eyes, chanting, as the train car became completely engulfed. Smoke filled the window.

Tess and everyone inside were screaming in terror. The heat soared. They were being left to burn alive.

More from panic than courage, Tess smashed her way out the rear doors, leaping over the flames. The fire caught hold of her, her hair burning, and Tess rolled on the snow. She caught a blurring look at the blind children, trapped behind her. They would never get out alone.

Rolling and thrashing, she conquered the fire on her body, but the children were screaming, with their lungs and their very souls.

She snatched up a blanket from the ground and began beating at the fire.

An ice scarecrow.

It was a simple figure carved upon a nearly hidden frame, some artist's handiwork.

And it was all that greeted Tobias as they reached the town of Blackthorne. Not a soul joined them. The little city was empty, or nearly so. There was one man's upright body, propped up strangely on the town gates, his distorted face covered in ice. He was all that remained of the villagers, it would seem.

Tobias swallowed, unnerved, pondering a way to make light of the grim scenario facing them. He could think of nothing to say.

Their expressions taut with fear, they continued on, making their way into town. It was nothing more than one street, a huddling of ancient wooden buildings against the wilderness, some abandoned horse carriages here and there.

New structures had yet to be built around these original edifices, though the fresh paint and restored wooden stairways testified to the efforts of the development committee. In the distance, other plain, early American homes, all of them white, each as simple as a folk painting or any child's drawing of a house, lay spread out in clearings, overseeing dead farms. Blackthorne had been a town with little to offer, it seemed, except that it was not Salem.

A furious banging drew their attention to a stable, where Tobias could make out several terrified horses, three or perhaps four, kicking deliriously as the men passed.

Everywhere there were signs of WELCOME and ICE SKATES FOR RENT. At the street's end, a collection of ice-sculpted scarecrows fronted the icy church.

"What's happening here . . . ?" whispered Sattler.

Not a sound met them, just the wind.

They plodded toward the ice church. It was a grand creation, snow and ice sculpted into a classic building of worship, a respectable ten feet high, and steepled.

Tobias's eyes slipped over it quickly, but a new current of feeling took his attention.

Slowly, Tobias turned toward one of the old white houses nearby. "Someone's in there," he said hesitantly.

He knew he was right. Human emotion, living feeling, had an unmistakable scent.

No one wanted to go in. Tobias at last started to move toward it, and the others followed. They closed in on the winter-beaten house.

Tobias eased the door open and went inside. Michael and Sattler came in behind him. Tobias could feel something alive before he could see it, his eyes adjusting to the darkness, scanning over rustic furniture, Indian artifacts . . .

. . . and a man hidden by the dark, staring back, sitting, his arms wrapped around a shotgun like a precious infant.

"Don't come in."

Everyone stood still.

"Just let me be."

All eyes were fixed nervously on the shotgun in the man's hand.

Tobias surprised everyone by stepping closer, gingerly. "What happened?"

The waiting man stared back, his face invisible in the dim light. "Something was killing us," he grunted. Tobias eased closer, trying to see the man's eyes. The man continued, in halting speech. "I blacked out. Then I . . . wandered around . . . It got so very cold . . . cold like I've never known. I came back in, and . . . there wasn't anyone here anymore." Tobias eased the shotgun away from the man, handed it to Sattler. Seeing the man's riding whip, he handed that away, too.

"You have a horse?" asked Tobias, friendly, calm.

"Out there somewhere."

Tobias nodded. The man wanted to talk, saying more without prompting. "I had started working with my brother; we brought up horses to sell. They never wanted to come. The horses. They knew. They knew this wasn't a right place. God in heaven . . . Everything went into wild disarray here. People were thrown around like puppets," he said, his teeth clenching.

Puppets, thought Tobias. Like that cheap and tawdry couple that had run from the train, like that lonely doctor in his house, all of them toys of Malgore. How does she do it? What means gives her such control?

The man in the chair went on. "Most of 'em died after a few

minutes. I don't know what it was . . . what it wanted from us. I never saw it directly. All I saw was rage. Absolute rage, God help us." He coughed.

Tobias looked at him carefully. "Are you sick, sir?"

The man looked back at him with vague distrust. "I've been fighting off black lung for some years."

Sattler asked, "You don't know where the people went?"

"Yeah, I think I do," said the man, rocking in his chair. "Can't go in there myself."

Tobias and the young men exchanged glances.

"I pray you'd tell us where they went, sir."

CHAPTER TWENTY-NINE

✥

A moment later Tobias and Sattler were outside. Tobias motioned for Michael to stay with the man, and he did so without complaint, turning back at the door.

Without a word, Tobias and Sattler headed toward the ice church.

Tobias felt numb. He'd been through too much, had been burned, inside and out, and wanted only to be done with this nightmare and be back with Tess, away from here, in New York, tuning his cello.

They trudged on, every step filling them with more fear.

"Maybe we could shove that man in there first and see what happens," Sattler said.

Tobias looked at him with a sidelong glance. "I can't say that I care for morbid humor."

Neither had the heart for talking any more, and soon they were standing in front of the ice church, speechless in the chill wind. There were no sounds from the building.

"We don't have to do this," Sattler pointed out finally.

"We've checked everything here. This is the only place left to look for help."

Sattler thought for a moment. "Tobias. This is madness. We both know this is madness. Is there some piece I'm missing?"

Tobias was fixated on the church. "There's something I have to see in there."

"I'm quite certain there's nothing we want to see inside that."

"I have to finish what was started. I have to see their belongings returned to them. I think this is where they were hanged."

"It's not yours to do." Sattler stared at him. "This is insane."

"We need to see this through. I need to do this for them. It may be the way to kill that thing." For just a second Tobias had begun to feel unsure.

Sattler studied the building nervously. "The door of the church looks like the den of an animal. It feels very much like a trap to me. We've survived this long; we can find another way. Why do you force us ahead like this?"

Tobias tried to see into the opening at the ice church. The mystery called to him. But it was more than temptation—there'd be no chance for any of them if he couldn't find a method to kill Malgore.

"It's trickery of some kind," said Sattler. "You know it. It's too weak now to attack us, so it lures us inside and seals us in. Then it waits to regain its power."

"There's a logic to what you say."

"Look here, forget all of this. Let's turn around, let's just get some horses and keep going," said Sattler, intense now. "You've seen enough death."

To his surprise, Tobias nodded slowly. "Yes."

"Right. All right, then. You want to live, don't you?"

Tobias looked at him, deeply thoughtful. "Yes. Turns out I do." He was in a state of slight disbelief at his own words.

Sattler handed him the horsewhip. "Let's get a horse and get out of here."

He made it sound so simple.

To the surprise of both of them, Tobias took the offering. He looked ahead, to the most prominent scarecrow made of ice, stalactites hanging over its empty sockets. He found some final answer somewhere in those eyes, and he turned away from the winter-made church.

But it was too late.

Without warning, from the scarecrow's downturned mouth came a shock of sound and wind, and the two men were dropped by the force of it.

Falling into a sleep, Tobias felt his body scraped along as if by the wind.

He was being swallowed by the ice church.

Tess had helped the children out of the burning railway car, but they had run from the fire in terror, without thinking and had been separated, gotten lost in the storm.

Tess could see the train car still burning in the snow.

Her refuge was gone. She was in the open.

She looked around. Amid the rows of trees, she saw the blind boys, each alone, wandering, stumbling; the lone survivors. Tess felt her heart drop at the sight of them all, a responsibility she had never wanted.

The snow relented, revealing, as she turned around, the doctor's estate—the long, tall old house and its smaller partner. The biggest building was a burned-out, ancient hulk, the old refuge of the Salem runaways. She hated the idea of returning to the room with the corpse. But it was shelter.

Tess stared at it, distrustful. She looked back, up in the trees, to the darkening evening sky. Everywhere it seemed there was a threat from the forest.

She realized she always counted on Tobias to help her with such decisions, and at the same moment, the fact hit her that he always allowed the final judgment to be hers. She allowed him to tug at her, because she wanted it—there was truly no manipulation at all.

She had no notion of how long she stood there, thinking about it.

"Boys . . . ," she whispered, and then even quieter, "come with me."

CHAPTER THIRTY

A twisting snake of smoky blue mist had hold of Tobias and Sattler, pulling them into the ice church. It took time, for the misty form of Wilhelm was weak, but the young men did not resist. Their bodies made sloppy grooves in the snow.

Tobias opened his eyes groggily, feeling the sliding motion, but he had no power over his muscles. He could not run. And he was desperate. Something was now approaching. He saw a blurred, creeping figure in the windswept snow, slowly and confidently moving toward the church doorway.

Malgore.

Tobias felt his body dragged away from her and rolled into the church entry, and Sattler was pulled in beside him. As he saw the witch approaching in an unhurried, arrogant stride, Tobias realized the protective mist was building up around the doorway, and Wilhem's barely visible fingers were now collapsing the icy entryway. Malgore could not enter.

The spirit had saved him again.

Malgore leaped and scaled the top of the ice church in an angry rush.

The creature pondered its next move from the rooftop.

Beyond the guarding ice scarecrows—their arms stretched out in icy crucifixion—the witch considered how to enter . . . or whether it was even necessary. . . .

Inside the ice church, Tobias and Sattler awoke in a hallway.

Very little light entered from either direction. There was no way to know which way was out. Heading down the hall, they passed a few flickering lanterns, frozen into the ground. It was too much effort to break one loose.

Silently they walked on, deeper into a blackness so richly devoid of light Tobias felt himself near despair as it stretched on.

"Are you there?" Sattler called.

"Stay with me," Tobias answered. "I'm right up ahead of you."

"Tobias . . . ?"

"Keep coming."

They made slow progress. Then Tobias stopped in fear. He felt as if a man were breathing upon him mere inches ahead, a sour exhale coming out of the darkness. Tobias could feel it on his eyelashes, his skin . . . sickly breath, and anger in it, somehow. Tobias didn't move, waiting. But the man did not lash out, did not speak, and Tobias's muscles relaxed. He wondered if it was his imagination. Or the spirit of Wilhelm, now angering?

The feeling quickly faded, and Tobias kept going, groping forward, hands out, a sadly feeble defense.

Then they could see just the tiniest strands of light, and emerged into a narrow ice hallway dimly lit with lamps. They continued on into a chamber, where several beautiful six-foot ice angels surrounded a large ice fountain, with frozen water forming arches from the spouts. Champagne glasses waited at the base of the fountain.

Carved into the ice at the entryway a sign said: WHERE OLD MAN WINTER PREYS.

It must have seemed amusing at one time.

Tobias and Sattler crossed past it, into the dark hallway beyond.

It was twilight now.

Tess led the trail of children, all clasping hands, through the snow.

"Hurry, hurry, come now," Tess urged the boys.

They entered the smaller house, but Tess could not stomach the sight of the dead doctor inside, with his ice-burned, sickly colored face. She immediately turned to leave again, when the rustling of pages stopped her.

A small book lying in the center of the room was being paged through, rustling from an invisible force. And then the doctor's dead hands were tugged by an azurelike mist as if he were reaching, as if to indicate the tattered volume.

Tess went to it quickly. She was surprised to realize it was the witch-hunter's journal, left behind by Wilder in his scuffle with the doctor, and her eyes fell to the handwritten words over an illustration of Old Widow Malgore, apparently torn from another volume and pasted here.

Tess read the writing carefully, "Many ways of . . . killing . . . Assured of death . . ."

"What is it?" asked one of the boys, standing fearfully at the door with the others.

Tess kept her eyes on the book, whispering more to herself than him. "It changed over the years . . ."

"What did?"

"The rhyme," said Tess, reading Josiah Jurey's notes. "Not 'dance upon the grave . . .' It was once 'Old Widow Malgore, never had a grave.' '. . . Old Widow Malgore, her heart is made of wicker, Old Widow Malgore, it must be burned to flicker . . .' '"

The nursery rhyme held a message, distorted over the years.

It was a method for killing the witch.

Unnerved by the quiet, Tobias continued with Sattler. Finally they emerged in the circular main chamber of the ice church, where dozens of men stared back at them in welcome.

For a moment, Tobias was taken aback. But then he realized they did not blink. They were gathered, pressed together on one side of the icy room, just standing, staring.

Dead.

Tobias could feel the sadness of their lost lives, like half-remembered music, and he knew that he would no longer see human emotion as a plaything. He let his eyes track over to the large center of the round room, where three old men dressed in suits, perhaps the town fathers, were standing there, spaced apart, near an altar covered in frost. At the altar knelt a bearded man made of ice, near an icy placard that read OLD MAN WINTER.

Tobias saw something more alarming and strange, like no experience he'd ever had with the spirit world.

The image of Father Winter shaped into the ice was unnervingly familiar.

His father's face lay before him in ice, sculpted to look exactly as it had in the séance in New York—but, then, slowly Tobias's eyes began to make out the sculpture's true appearance. He gazed upon a fanciful incarnation of Winter itself, and nothing more. His heart beat furiously. Some cruel magic it was, or some sad twist in his psychology.

Deeper into the room he could now dimly see women lying dead, like broken toys. Tobias pondered all of this in horror.

Sattler whispered, stunned. "She killed them all."

Tobias turned to him. "Why . . . ? Why this hate?" And how could she have created this figure to taunt him, weaken him? Just as she had summoned the elk here from the north for sustenance, could her potency reach beyond any boundaries?

The room grew misty with a fullness like smoke. He heard his father moaning from the emptiness. "Good-for-nothing," said the voice. "Left me for dead. Dead like you always wanted. Bloodsucking little vermin."

The face of Winter remained eerily placid.

Tobias took a few steps back and felt tears sting his eyes. The passing illusion was overwhelmingly strong, a cherished voice from childhood, warped here into something vicious.

He had no time to make sense of it. A glance at Sattler proved it was all in Tobias's mind, for his companion seemed to have seen and heard nothing. He wondered what trickery Sattler was enduring within his own head.

Sattler remained staring at the sight of the killings, shaking, and Tobias had to take his satchel from him.

"The spirit wants what is his . . . ," said Tobias, and he placed the box of Puritan possessions—the rings, the dress pieces, all that Wilhelm and Abigail left behind—into the ice near the altar, burying it hurriedly.

"It has protected us . . . ," Tobias said, in bitter prayer. "It shall again . . ."

But ice chips were raining down from the ceiling. It was breaking up. A loud, brutish drumming resounded from above.

"That Thing is coming for us," Sattler said. "We came here for nothing. We left the women . . . behind . . ."

Tobias whispered in a broken voice, "It has meant nothing." Sattler looked vacantly at him. Nothing emerged from the buried box. No magic came from it, and Tobias stood in disbelief. The spirit was not going to help them. The icy structure was quaking, splintering. . . . .

And suddenly part of the ceiling *shattered*, and breaking through from the hole, Malgore fell upon Tobias, knocking him to the ground, his face pushed into the ice.

Sattler slammed his torch onto her head, and Malgore spun, charging him to the wall.

Tobias weakly rose, grabbing the long crescent dagger from his pocket, and began jabbing at the Thing's back, hard, quickly, again and again.

Malgore screamed and pulled away, falling back into the arms of the Old Man Winter sculpture.

In that moment, the spirit of Wilhelm took shape vaguely, and began to drive the entire sculpture back, bashing the witch's head against the wall. The spirit *was* here. Tobias stabbed the dagger a last time into Malgore's heart, and those animal eyes locked onto his, stunned, fixated. . . .

In the doctor's house, Tess read from Josiah's book feverishly, voraciously. "Burn the body, burn the body . . ."

She looked up, absorbing the words.

Old Widow Malgore, her heart must burn . . . to flicker.

It was fire. Fire would kill the witch.

But the creature called Malgore was already dead.

Tobias and Sattler looked exhaustedly at their work. The witch—a spindly albino form, a skeletal figure—lay splayed against the statue of ice.

The spirit's misty coils knocked over a lamp, starting a meager fire.

But Tobias turned and kicked snow over it. "Get the other lantern. Let's get out of here."

They moved to leave—but the witch was disentangling itself behind them, rising to come after them, though they did not yet know it. It had disguised its emotion, and Tobias felt nothing, walking on, as the wretch closed in on them.

"Tess will think the worst . . . ," Tobias started to say—but suddenly Sattler was yanked backward, his neck breaking as the witch-creature threw him against the ice sculpture.

Horror filled Tobias. Furious, Malgore lifted the entire sculpture of Old Man Winter, and crushed it down on Tobias with great force. He fell like a doll, as Malgore screeched, pushing down upon the statue.

The pressure created a crater in the ground, where Tobias lay motionless beneath the ice carving. His eyes fluttered shut.

Malgore regarded her work, and screeched again.

CHAPTER THIRTY-ONE

Tess watched as the indefinite form of the Puritan girl lifted Josiah Jurey's book and soared from the room, heading outside, leading Tess and the children to the large main house.

An instant later the bolted doors there rattled open.

"What is this . . . ?" one child asked, as they entered.

It was hard for Tess to know how to answer; the spirit had lost its energy, and was out of sight completely.

It was a weary shelter at best. The windows were gone, and the cold wind howled inside. Tess dropped one of the blind boy's hands, and he fumbled for hers, terrified. "Don't, don't let go."

"I'm sorry." She took it again, and they all stood together for a long moment, out of breath and out of courage.

"Did you hear that?" one of the boys said.

Tess stiffened in fear, having heard nothing. Were their sensitive ears picking up more than she could?

"It's above us," said another boy.

She looked up. "There's nothing."

"I heard it. Something's here. Something's right above us," said the first boy, pulling back from Tess.

"Stop, stop. There's nothing there. I'll prove it to you," said Tess, alarming them more. She dropped the boy's hand again, and moved toward the stairs, trying to believe the gentle spirit was the cause of the noise.

"Stay here," she said, steeling herself.

The boys' faces clearly showed their terror, but they had few choices. They might have to be here for a time, and Tess wanted to know it was safe. She went up the wide staircase cautiously, her head cocked, listening.

Finally she began to hear something, a distant calling, as she rose. She was close to finding the source; it was like a melody being played just beyond several closed doors. She climbed to the upstairs hallway in darkness.

Then she stopped in sudden terror, able to go no farther.

She turned to run back—but she was *sucked up ten feet into the darkness.* Taken.

Tobias awoke and clawed his way out of the crater inside the ice church, frantic.

He believed the witch was gone. Left him for dead.

Sattler's body lay broken beside him.

As his eyes fell upon the young man, he felt a profound and terrible guilt. Tobias could have been more careful. He knew more about the threat in these woods. He should have been the one to die.

He was trapped. He looked up at the hole Malgore had created in the ceiling, and, with difficulty, climbed to it by scaling the sculpture and the ragged wall, pulling his body up with all his strength into the colder world outside.

Twilight was fading. In the upstairs bedroom, Tess stood, her body tense. In the dim light, she could see small animals—dead goats and other creatures—hanging from hooks, strange writing scrawled on the walls, and carved on the floors, and as she leaned forward . . .

A pit. It was built into the floor and led into a red-black throat of fire. It was deeper than seemed possible, ringed with human bones, torn spines, dried flesh.

Tess pulled at a long metal meat hook that clung to the pit, and, trembling, realized it had blood on it.

She had learned exactly what this meant from Josiah's book: She held the weapon that could kill the wretch. If the body was then burned, the witch would be destroyed. A simple arithmetic arranged itself in Tess's mind.

She felt old desiccated feelings running into her arm from the hook, the emotions of the tortured now muted by time, and in the room around her, pain and misery from far too many deaths. She was in Widow Malgore's den. Its horrors would stay with her forever. She pocketed the vile hook and stood up, shaking.

And then her eyes met another's.

In the empty, burned room, a female figure stood before her.

Tess whispered tearfully, "Abigail."

The ghost was only partially lit, her face veined and pale. Her features began to dissolve, the flesh around her eyes drooping, the bones of her cheeks falling, her countenance altering itself bit by bit until the woman that stood before Tess was a flickering, magic-lantern version of her own mother.

"Tess," the figure whispered. "Why do you stand there staring like a doll?"

It was her mother's voice, but not her style of speaking.

"Knew you'd abandon me. You lived up to every fear I ever had."

"Mother?"

"Every fear I ever had. What's the song? 'Lock her up in London Tower, lock her up'?"

The vision turned partially incorporeal, as if fighting to appear human, its fading voice whispery and weakening, barely understandable. "Always damaged goods. Always afraid of your own shadow," she murmured. "Never locked *you* up, did I? You made that choice."

Why was Abigail bringing this vision to her? Was she allowing her mother to speak through her, beyond the grave? *Could* Abigail do this?

"Daughter of mine . . ."

Then her mother's face vanished. Abigail returned. In a slow, steady pace she approached, broke apart into frost and mist, and fell inside Tess. She strained to hear Abigail's voice inside her, but the voice could not be heard; witchery had silenced it, even in death.

The spirit had grown desperate, her message swallowed before it could be learned. They could not communicate.

Instead Tess felt emotion vanish, until she was no longer taking in the pain and suffering around her. The spirit was giving her strength. Strength to face the unstoppable.

Tobias stumbled out into the evening as the fog flew in a violent wind around him. He ran, driven on by Wilhelm's power, past the house that Michael was in. The door lay open. Tobias stared in disgust. Malgore had killed them all.

He turned, rushing into the street.

The air cleared ahead, to reveal a desperate, tethered horse at the stable.

Salvation.

Tess shivered as ice entered her veins. The ghostly Abigail had told her all that she could, half whispers that had floated into her from the world of death. There was a threat in what she felt and heard: *Kill the wretch, or we shall kill you.*

Had the vision of her mother been some kind of angry warning?

There was no more time to think. The ghost's voice announced clearly, "She is here."

Tess was looking at darkness. There was nothing there at all. Her blood warmed. Abigail had lost the strength to remain with her.

A shape moved behind Tess, approaching, she was aware of it though she didn't see it. Oldness washed over her, a smell of rot and sense of ancient resentment, a hollowness that she had come to recognize as the witch. It was coming.

Tess stared straight ahead into the dim room but could not see Malgore at all.

Instead, she saw Abigail, still struggling to appear, trying to warn her. Then Tess heard something behind her.

She tried to move, but was suddenly forced to her knees by an unseen magic. Lightning crackling upon her skin, she crawled, moving under an invisible weight, as behind her the mist spread and rushed the hallway, making a milky dust of the blue evening light.

Ahead of Tess through a hallway window came the silhouette of the new arrival. She watched the figure slip in, the shockingly lithe and supernaturally thin creature. Widow Malgore had returned home.

The witch rushed toward Tess and screeched maniacally, grabbing hold of the smoke-blue mist, as if it could be crushed.

But the mist had life, and thickness in her hand. It fought to free itself. . . .

And Tess knew she was seeing two kinds of forces in battle.

CHAPTER THIRTY-TWO

＊

Malgore's face contorted, fangs springing forth, a
screeching let loose from her throat. Desperately Tess
crawled away to get downstairs, as the mist obscured
any glimmer of evening light from outside.

Tess screamed, as Malgore tore apart the blue, mistlike gossamer
strings, and then continued, relentless, after Tess.

Malgore crept downstairs almost like a spider, bestial, with long
spindly arms and legs. The thorns that were her teeth gnashed
repeatedly.

The witch shoved Tess farther down the stairs.

But suddenly—the mist-spirit rushed at Malgore, washing her
aside, toppling her off the stairway.

The room was suddenly in darkness.

Tobias rode from Blackthorne on horseback. He stared straight
ahead, intent on not looking back, not thinking anything but
move, move, move. . . .

Moonlight struggled in. Tess fought to awaken. She had fallen
at the middle of the stairway, and had stayed there, unconscious.

Exhausted to its core, her body still wanted sleep. But she heard the boys calling to her; they needed her, there was no one else.

Downstairs, she had to move past the collapsed body of Malgore, and as her legs crossed past those withered fingers of knotted bone, she saw them twitch. The Thing was awakening. Its claws still had hold of a blue silken mist. Its grip was tightening. Panicked, Tess felt her leg rub past the white mane of Malgore's hair, and she suddenly heard the witch breathing, speaking.

Tess reached the boys, grabbing the first one's hand.

He was screaming. "What is happening—"

She had to get them all outside.

"Link hands," she screamed. She pulled them out into the snow. She glanced back, seeing Malgore crouching in dim light, chanting, but the blue-tinged spirit in the witch's claws tore loose. The witch howled, then began rising in rage, as the mist expanded. They left the house in the distance but she could still see light, pale blue from the swirling mist at the ceilings, Abigail's frenetic spirit, pouring out. Tess stared, transfixed. The boys were running, stumbling, trying to get away. Tess grabbed hold of one student, but the children were too scattered now. Gathering them was like catching birds.

"Follow my voice," she called, backing into the woods. "Come with me."

They made their way to the sound. She was rounding them up. Just another minute and she'd have them. She stared back at the abandoned building.

From out of the dead house, the illuminated mist became a female figure entering the night. It was Abigail, gathering the last of her strength; Tess could see her in a long cloak, fleeing, the most alive and most substantial the spirit had ever appeared, made solid and corporeal by sheer desperation. Tess's heart leaped in fear for her. Striding from the house, just after the girl, there came a vague, deformed shape—Malgore—quick, but with an unnatural, hobbling gait.

Tess saw the Thing snatch Abigail. It had her, like a fish on a hook. And just as helpless, she flailed.

The Thing reached into her, reached into her back, and its fingers closed around her spine.

Abigail screamed soundlessly. The witch could not kill her, but it could punish her, send pain to her with a devilish magic, her most cherished form of torture. And Abigail fell apart, hearing her Mother shrieking with a voice part animal, part woman, in some indefinable way.

Tess stared as Abigail's form dissipated into strands, drifting through the forest, nothing more than mist and wind.

The witch-thing shivered with uncontrolled bloodlust.

Tess let out a moan.

The wretch looked up—eyes flashing red—it had found her.

Tobias squinted hard as he rode through the snowfall. His horse shot past a fallen tree near the rails, and behind him the snow breathed upon him in a fast-traveling wall of wind. He was being pushed onward. In his head he became aware of Tess again, sensing her far ahead of him, drawing him like the tide to the shore. She was out there somewhere, and he would find her.

★ ★ ★

Tess's eyes fixed on a figure in the distance behind her and she begged herself to look away, but could not.

The wretch, half buried in darkness, was snarling a call. Her massive cat crawled from the blackness. Malgore snapped a whip brutally, slashing its eye. The animal moved to her, low and whimpering, a thing of flesh and bone.

Tess tore herself loose from the mesmerizing sight, and she led the group away. She had recovered all the boys, but there was nowhere to go, they were just running, directionless.

Snowdrift surrounded them. Ethereal light began weaving behind it: a vast flying ghost, like a mirage swimming through the air, rattling trees. Abigail.

Tess felt the spirit's emotion, *You have failed us. You have failed us.*

CHAPTER THIRTY-THREE

ess brought the children back to the train tracks, where the dim hulks of the ruined cars lay waiting. And now the ghostly figure—its shape coming together, tightening—descended, a glassy spirit Tess could barely see in the darkness.

The spirit began to circle the children. Tess couldn't move.

"Let go, let go, it doesn't want us," cried one boy, pulling free of her. "It wants *you*."

"You have to go with me," Tess cried to the boys, terrified to the bone.

She stood alone now. The spirit closed in on her, its dim face visible. The ghostly shape—it was somehow still feminine—soared around Tess, smelling her, sensing her, preparing to strike.

Out from the veil of snow, Tobias, on horseback, came speeding into view.

Everything was healed in that split second. He swept by, grasping her hand, pulling her onto the horse, as behind him the wind dissipated the ghostly form of Abigail and battered the trees ferociously. Something had driven her away.

The horse reared onto its back legs, screeching in terror.

Malgore rode from the darkness on her immense jaguar beast.

The witch roared, right along with her familiar. As she passed, her grotesque arm slashed Tobias from his horse, which panicked. Tess grasped wildly to hold on.

The couple fell to the ground.

Instantly, Malgore's clawed hand closed around Tobias's face. He struggled to breathe as Tess screamed. She had lived to see him die.

The witch dragged him, dropped him, then stood, raising a long, curving knife to destroy him. But all of a sudden Malgore screamed, letting loose a terrible wailing. Tess had come from behind, stabbing the metal hook into her back, and out, tearing at the wretch.

Tess hissed, breathlessly, "Your weapon—" and as Malgore turned, Tess plunged it into her heart. "*Yours.*" She executed the move perfectly, just as the witch-hunter had instructed her in the book. She was stunned at herself.

Malgore stumbled back, gasping.

The huge, horrific shape of her body was blown back as if it were nothing but a sack of skin. Tobias reached for the curved knife—and they fought for it, the witch fighting for life with brazen intensity.

Tobias wrenched the long knife free—and swung it into Malgore's thin midsection, nearly bisecting the witch with a single blow. The wretch came apart like old dust and dried bone, still thrashing in death.

Tess reached for a boy's fallen lantern and hurled it at the witch's heart, and fire burst upon the body. The witch-creature writhed in flames. Still afire, it crawled toward Tess, though weakened and dying.

The jaguar creature saw this—and rushed in—its huge jaws closing on Malgore's head and thrashing about, exacting its revenge, as nearby the horse jolted madly, neighing in fright. *Old Widow Malgore, she keeps a devil slave . . .*

And then the black predator pulled her remains into the darkness, disappearing into its domain.

It would devour the witch.

Old Widow Malgore, your devil will break free . . . and vengeance you will see . . .

Tobias ran with Tess toward the tracks as fast as they could.

Tess glanced back and was astonished. From the darkness a torrent of vague shapes were flowing downward—swooping in upon the witch's corpse—and breaking it into fiery pieces as the wind grew.

The long-dead phantoms of this place, held here by the witch's power, wanting revenge for their unholy deaths, were at last receiving it.

But there was something yet unfinished. Both Tess and Tobias felt a deadness behind them, and they turned to see one of the blind boys slowly engulfed in light-blue mist, his eyes clouded with the same subtle color. A hard, malignant male voice came oozing out of him.

"Thou hast done us a service," said the boy.

Tobias and Tess looked at him in fear.

"Know you this: she held our tongue 'til now," the boy said, and his face briefly flashed with light but there was a calm to him, and to the moment as well. "We were hoping for you. You are special among all others. Your fine gifts are a blessing to us as well."

The boy's hands at his side worked nervously. "You've been made tender for it, over the years. Possession . . . is no easy thing to endure. The body fights it . . . but not yours." His voice broke apart as he coughed. His breathing was labored.

Possession. Tobias stared in disbelief. "You wanted us . . ."

"We want what anyone would. To be flesh and blood again."

It was Wilhelm.

Tess watched the boy step closer, his eyes glazed, not his own.

"All we wanted was to be together. Denied by everyone. Denied by her," said Wilhelm, speaking through the boy in that burning voice. "We would not be damned to live as spirits forever. We would take hold of new bodies, have a life free of this torture. But her mother was always here. Always, she killed the flesh before we could take it . . ."

The boy's face began to stretch, as if another face were underneath. The blind child choked, and the spirit was unleashed out of him, tunneling toward Tobias.

Abigail's shape came from behind and knocked Tess to the ground, as a frost settled upon them both.

"Fight them—Tess—"

Tobias got no other words out.

He braced himself. Eyes tight, he shook his head; it was like a swarm of bees inside him, his brain fighting against it, and finally, the mist pushed harder, ramming him into a thick tree.

He hit the ground gasping. He could no longer feel the world around him, or hear it. Something was in his head, searching, rifling through memories and dreams and emotions and thoughts, looking for a way to drive him further into fear, to scare him truly out of his mind.

He felt it find a place inside, where he kept the pain over his mother and father's deaths. Tobias had lived through the theater fire, and his guilt for surviving shone brightly among his memories. He had ached to know why he hadn't been killed, and the spirit inside him took hold of this bit of him and crushed it until he felt a flood of emotion—sorrow, hopelessness—and the spirit wanted him to feel it, wanted him to want to die.

Tobias felt himself becoming the Wilhelm ghost. He lost any sense of his bond with Tess. She was gone from him, and he couldn't fight anymore.

For Tess, there was nothing but a searing blue-white incandescence in her vision and filling her senses. She fell, as the mist invaded her tiny frame, and she clenched her eyes shut, fighting it.

Tess knew Abigail's spirit wanted her. It was searching Tess, tearing through her subconscious, battering at her beliefs, driving her to the sense that she was nothing, had nothing, did not even deserve to exist. It was like a frightening, repeating music, and Tess could feel the triumph, of the wraith inside her.

All that she was, everything she'd ever been, was about to be stripped of her flesh and bone. She would join her mother and father, the ones she had left in that theater in New York, left to the agony of the fire while she had run.

With her eyes blinded, she listened hard to know if Tobias

had made it through alive—if she knew this, it would give her some strength, perhaps enough to fight back. . . .

It was morning now. The sun was rising.

Tess's eyes lifted to Tobias, who knelt down, embracing her.

"It's all right, we've made it, we've made it through," he was telling her, but she could hardly hear him, her heart was thundering so hard. He took her face in his hands, gently. "It's all right."

Tess was breathless, almost giddy, laughing in disbelief, "We're alive . . ."

He kissed her, desperate with relief.

As they kissed, the wind blew ice across the ground. It cut into them deeply, maliciously, to remind them who they were, and then it settled.

It was over.

The blind boys had fallen to the ground a distance away, huddled down in the storm, survivors, useless to the spirits.

Far off, the lamp of the train engine finally faded in the snow.

CHAPTER THIRTY-FOUR

He had questions but no answers.

The police officer watched Tess Goodraven sitting quietly on the seat in front of him. She had hardly spoken throughout the questioning.

The rescuers had taken the blind children into safe custody in an empty residence in Blackthorne. They had placed Tess in one room, Tobias in another, for there were serious concerns that something involving the occult had happened.

They were the only true eyewitnesses to survive.

And they were not talking.

Tobias Goodraven proved no more helpful than his youthful wife. The two of them seemed to have had their fill of horrors, and asked only to move on.

"If they are victims of something, what are they victims of?" asked the policeman. "Was there something in the forest that . . . lost its strength after the storm?"

Tobias looked off into the distance.

"I don't know how to ask about any of this," said the policeman, embarrassed to confront the question. "I suppose I'm asking if there's such a thing as ghosts."

"There is but one thing I know of ghosts."

Carefully, the constable watched Tobias's empty expression.

"There are two kinds," Tobias Goodraven went on. "Ones who want to make their peace with life and move on. And those who want life so badly they'll do anything to get it again."

The constable replied, "Did you see something out there, Mr. Goodraven? The only other survivors, of course, saw nothing. So we rely on you. *Were* these murders?"

"If indeed there be spirits here . . . they could no more be blamed for these deaths than a child for breaking his toys. They meant no more harm than a storm passing over."

Tobias stopped talking, and allowed the policeman to stare at him. "I've heard from people in Salem that you have a vile sense of humor, Mr. Goodraven, and if you're being funny . . . ," he said severely. "There are bodies out there; we've lost near a hundred souls today."

"They might've lost their bodies. They didn't lose their souls," Tobias said. "Fear not for them."

And that was all he said. The policeman let Tobias out into the hall, and Tess came out with the officer who had questioned her. They all moved away to confer as Tobias and Tess joined hands— nerves frayed, tired and relieved.

They heard one policeman say, "I'm not sure what they remember. They're just so very disturbed. . . ."

The men looked toward the couple.

Several male rescue workers entered at the door, one carrying a shattered cello, the second, a case. "I got them out," the first man said proudly. "One of them came through in serviceable shape."

He motioned to the intact cello case and looked at Tess solemnly. "I'm sure this meant a lot to you. Would you want to take it with you now?"

Tess eyed it emotionlessly. "No," she said, for it no longer held any meaning to her. It was a thing of the past, an outdated prop Tess Goodraven no longer needed to smooth out the jagged edges of life.

Outside, Tobias and Tess moved past the rescue workers, safe at last.

EPILOGUE

❦

Tess and Tobias Goodraven settled in Salem, their new home, their new beginning, after all the chaos.

They took a small apartment, and it was enough for them, with a window view of the city in the growing light of spring.

To watch them on a typical evening, one would say they needed little from life except each other's company. Every night Tobias and Tess sat down for a meal together. The room would be quiet, often somber.

Then Tobias would look up and talk to Tess.

He would speak German.

She would answer him, saying something about the richness of the food they were eating, and she'd go to the kitchen, bringing back tea. They would appear to be an ordinary couple at home, enjoying simple pleasures, except for one thing.

He might stare at his hand, pondering the lines there that he had not made, and she might take his hand in hers, as she sat beside him.

She might say—in German, of course, "Feels good to touch you again, after so long . . ."

The room would grow colder, and they might look up ominously at something almost beyond consciousness, something there just for a moment ... as books were rattled off the shelves ... as dust was blown from the windowsill of a closed window. The two would be staring ahead as ghostly strains of cello music would cascade down around them. It would pass, and the two would prepare for another uncomfortable meal, alien in their own skins.

The haunted having become the haunters, Tess and Tobias were now only shadows in this world, spectres whose unseen eyes would bear down upon those who had taken their flesh to possess as their own.

They'd stand there boldly, invisible and watchful. They had left behind their physical selves in that frigid land. And no one knew it.

Their lives had been stolen.

The couple at the table, the ones that called themselves Tess and Tobias Goodraven, would stare back blankly into the emptiness of the room.

These were not the same people who got on that train in Salem.

Only their bodies remained the same.